KISS

(

AN ANTHOLOGY

of

FLASH-FICTION

From the

WEST COUNTRY

by the

FLASH-FICTION

SOUTH WEST

WRITERS

Edited by Rachel Carter

Copyright © 2012

by Flash-Fiction South West

All rights reserved

Lulu Author

12795535

Kissing Frankenstein & Other Stories

Literature & Fiction

ISBN: 978-1-4716-8493-7

Published by Flash-Fiction South West

Printed by Lulu.com/gb

English

United Kingdom

ACKNOWLEDGEMENTS

Thank you to Natalie, Martha, Peter, Gail, Kay B, Kay W, Georgina, Tracy, Cath, Liz, Elizabeth, Amanda, Linda, Lorena and Noosh, for helping me with the initial reading stages. They have their own well-deserved section at the end of this book.

Thanks to everyone who has promoted this venture by way of tweeting, sharing links on the Internet and by word-of-mouth. And thanks to Gail for spreading the word in her local area.

Thanks to Calum for approaching me to be involved in National Flash Fiction Day and for supporting this west country anthology idea.

Thanks to Martha, Peter and everyone else who has been available to me for idea-bouncing.

A huge thank you goes to my mum, Liz Wood, for careful, non-invasive line-edits and who understands the importance of that fine balancing-act between creativity and accuracy

Rachel

FOREWORD

By Calum Kerr

"National Flash-Fiction Day" was what I typed into Google on 6th October 2011. It was National Poetry Day and I was jealous. I wanted to see if there was a Day that I could get involved with. I don't write poetry. I do write flash.

So I searched, but there was nothing, not even a sallow gathering in a darkened basement over at National Short Story Day. So, I asked around, I proposed the idea, I suggested, I cajoled, I pleaded and ordered, and finally... National Flash-Fiction Day was a reality. And what a reality! Readings, workshops, slams, flash-mobs, flash-points, flash-floods! And, of course, beautiful collections of words such as the one you have in your hand.

The above seems like I'm claiming all the credit for National Flash-Fiction Day. But it's not the case. The Day belongs to the writers taking part, it belongs to all of the authors in the book you're holding, and to its progenitor, Rachel Carter. And now... it belongs to you!

Enjoy the book, taste the morsels carefully, and relish their flavour. And then come over to www.nationalflashfictionday.co.uk and seek out some more.

Flash-fiction is…

'Short.'
'Moreish.'
'A concentrated story.'
'Like poison – effective in small doses.'
'Maybe a cross between fiction and poetry…?'

Flash-fiction is still a relatively new - and therefore "open" - genre. It has yet to be packaged up neatly into one definition with one set of rules. In my opinion, this is a good thing. It means there is a great variety of tiny fiction to be read and enjoyed. Writers are experimenting with the form and readers are enjoying the experience.

Some flash-fiction fans believe a flash-fiction should be a maximum of 300 words, others 500 words, some as much as 1,000 words. Some writers believe that because the form is short and fast that the writing time and approach should be short and fast.

In this collection are stories as short as 6 words and others that top nearly 1,000 words. A longer flash-fiction can be more like a short story, whilst there might be more "punch" from the briefer ones.

Are they like poetry?
Which length is best?
You decide…

CONTENTS

KISSING FRANKENSTEIN

&

OTHER STORIES

AUTOMORPH

I dived into the wineglass and swam a few strokes. The glass wrapped itself round me, then there was a cross noise and I was unceremoniously tipped out on to the floor.

The glass reformed itself and began:

'Lucky, huh! I might have been a sundae dish, or an ashtray, seriously shallow, eh? And then where'd you have been, tell me. Ambulance, A and E, head injury, that's what, you name it.'

'Sorry,' I said meekly, and wondered why it was me who was apologising. Somehow the new flexible and automorphing glass we all had nowadays didn't make life any easier and could be hard to cope with, especially when things went like this.

Even burglars, it was said, got told off when they tried to break windows: 'Push us aside, peel us back, bend us out, but don't even think of trying to break us. We don't break, us flexiglass windows.'

Bossy, uppish, trying to run the world, I thought. Even before today I'd known that the usual glassware, bowls and jugs in the kitchen could be very difficult. Better be careful.

'Really sorry,' I repeated and added idiotically – I could have kicked myself, though it would have been better to kick the wineglass – 'I hope you're OK, not … hurt or anything?'

'Hmmm.'

The glass wasn't going to be friendly, that was clear. It went on:

'You listen. Right now I'm a wineglass, red wine, white wine, whatever. But if I wanted I could'– there was a theatrical pause –'very quickly…' It speeded up: 'turn myself into a copita, one of those slender sherry glasses, know the ones I mean?' I nodded. 'Dive into me then, and you're a gonner: head down, drowning in amontillado, legs kicking, but not for long. And I might not take pity and help you out the next time.'

'No,' I agreed, as the pause lengthened. This was crazy, being scared of a glass.

'I don't think you're taking me seriously,' it said. 'We'll teach you.' It raised its voice. 'Guys, girls, all of you! Everyone out! We need to give someone a lesson.'

Out of the kitchen cupboards they poured, literally. The floor was awash with a flood of liquid glass. I could still move my feet, but they were heavy and getting heavier every second.

'Ever wondered how flies get trapped in amber?' laughed the glass, itself still in wineglass form, but beginning to melt and drip. 'Well, now you know.'

Muriel Higgins

NEW DAWN

I watch the sinking sun, a blood-shot ball exhausted by the long hot day. A million blades of grass irritate me through the thin cotton of my post-war trousers. I swear Lorna has stitched them from some salvaged tablecloth from the sideboard drawer.

I toss my sandwich crusts to the birds, their feathers frayed and singed by the war. The hills on the horizon seem guarded, as if a secret waits in their folds. They know when we will once more turn the world on its head and shake the loose change of good living out of its pockets.

I shield my eyes from the bloody horizon. The hills turn black. Black with memories of screaming birds scattering.

The birds have rediscovered their nests. And I have come home.

Home to find my Lorna's hands roughened and mottled from war-work and scrubbing and turning the soil. Our servants gone. Either dead or with new independence, working in factories where they run a line of machines instead of running back and forth at our command.

We're on our own now. Me in my seersucker trousers instead of my strong khaki. No men at my side. No gun in my hands. I feel like white blubber, awake in the deep-blue of the night with my grotesque dreams of hearts blistering like blooms from khaki shirts.

'Only one way to get these blighters. And that's to stand up and be counted.'

All my mates were called Tommy. No point remembering names now. And that was Tommy's last shout before he spun three times and flopped like a fish back into the trench.

And Lorna in her patched frock, holding me with her hardened hands. That's what I came back to. This is our new life. The cries of scorched birds, the flinty eyes of the brooding hills, servants' bells that will never be answered.

The sun drops into its slot, glad to be gone. I stand up and brush the crumbs from my trousers. I go home through fields still peppered with prisoners of war, berry-brown and flaxen-haired. Longing for home too.

We all wait together for the new dawn.

Joanna Campbell

ALMOST

From the way she scooped him from his buggy, shushed him, kissed his tears and hugged him all the way home, he might almost have been hers.

Martha Williams

BRIDGES

Jo had never told a soul that she had been terrified of wooden bridges for as long as she could remember. It was the thought of wood splintering. She was scared of water; never went swimming. Wooden bridges were just too close to the cold wetness that threatened to close over the top of her head, fill her lungs till they burst. Somehow, in spite of living in the countryside, she had managed to avoid ever walking on one. Concrete bridges, over roads, now she was fine with them.

When she heard the splash a few feet (plus a bridge-length) away from where she was walking, at first it didn't occur to her to try and *do* anything. Still, she couldn't resist having a look. She peered out from under her black fringe. There was a small-ish person wearing a khaki coat and a pink scarf thrashing about at the edge of the water. The parent was nowhere in sight. Probably one of those so-called mums she'd seen in the town centre, hair scraped back off their foreheads, cigarette ash dripping onto the snot-encrusted pallid faces of their child in a buggy. Jo was a terrible snob, and she knew it. She didn't want kids herself, ever. There wasn't a maternal bone in her skinny little well-dressed body. But that didn't mean she approved of people who had them and didn't look after them.

They always said (whoever *they* were) that it was possible to overcome fear in extreme situations – you heard stories of women doing crazy things to save their kids from danger. But this kid (the splashes seemed less frequent now – or was Jo imagining this?) wasn't *her* bloody kid and she wasn't prepared to step foot on the wooden, creaky, break-any-second-now-send-you-to-your-death slats, with god only knows what lurking under the bridge. She thought of trolls from childhood stories. Goats with trippy-trappy hooves. Thought of falling in. *Like that poor kid has, through no fault of its own.*

Someone else would have to sort it out, fish the unfortunate little bugger out by its coat. The problem was, and she was fast coming to realise this fact, that there was no Someone Else around. By the time Jo had finished thinking this thought, her brain had sent the message to her feet to stop moving. They were frozen, two useless lumps of meat at the end of her legs. She stood still for what seemed like a long time.

When the kid shouted 'Mummy' in a way that sounded so forlorn, so resigned to its fate of drowning alone in a dirty river, it was like a slap round the face by someone a lot more sensible and, let's face it, caring than Jo was.

You selfish cow, a child is drowning over there and you're pandering to your silly fears. Get a grip.

She walked over to the bridge, placed a shaking hand on it, lifted her right foot onto the steps. Heart thudding, she placed one foot in front of the other. *Easy-peasey, lemon-squeezy!*

One step at a time, Joanna! This won't hurt a bit.

God knows how, but she made it to the other side without being sick and the bridge (the world) didn't fall in after all.

Louisa Adjoa Parker

LITTLE BUG

He found her on the streets, wandering as lost and free as a ghost. He sat in the car smoking a roll-up and watched as she weaved through the legs of figures hunched against the wind. And when she looked at him, eyes-wide, he knew he didn't ever want to let her go.

'Let me bring you in from the cold,' he said, 'for the winters are harsh here in Russia. Some say maidens are frozen to statues of white ice.'

So he brought her in from the cold and into a place where people rushed to and fro; there were others here too, taken from those same streets.

He fed her sweetmeats and pieces of ham and chicken and they gave her many names: *Kudryavka, Laika, Little Lemon*, but to him she was always his *Zhuchka*, his Little Bug. She tried strange new foods, squeezed into small spaces and ran for miles without leaving the compound. When the scientists went home at night they all paced their pens and whined.

And finally it was time to choose. The winds and snows had given way to green fields and brown soil. And he knew there had never really been any choice: Little Bug ran the fastest, jumped the highest, squeezed into the smallest spaces.

'You should be proud of your little Kudryavka,' said his supervisor.

He shook hands and accepted back-slaps. Little Bug was inspecting him through the thin wire of her pen, her white feet placed neatly together. That night he brought her home into the warm and let her play with his children.

'Pappa, can we keep her?'

He watched the dog standing on her hind legs. They tied blue ribbon round her neck and made her a bed of odd bits of cloth – outgrown dresses and itchy jumpers. In the morning they wrapped her in blankets for the journey. As he drove past the small grey houses, and then the brown and yellow landscape, he often watched Little Bug in the rear-view mirror. Part of him hoped she'd see a rabbit or squirrel, and she'd jump out of the moving car. But she didn't. She sat with her tongue lolling as the world slid by and when he stopped the engine she wagged her tail.

And then he sent her back into the cold once more. He thought about what a thing it was to exist only in the moment; all she'd know would be noise, darkness and then a terrible heat. And perhaps she'd look at Earth and wonder at its beauty, but probably not.

He told his children she'd become the brightest star. But sometimes in the middle of the night he stood outside his small house, in the garden his wife tended each Sunday, and looked up at the sky. He thought about many things in those hours before dawn, before the birds began their morning chorus. And on some nights he thought about his Little Bug and how far she'd come.

Claire Huxham

MEETING, PARTING

Is it really twenty-six years?

We both say, 'You look just the same.'

What is it we recognise in each other? For we both wear time's signs of age.

The connection is there, our conversation intense. So much to say, yet you tell me you never normally talk like this. Of late, nor do I; I find it hard to recall when words meant so much. Your eyes smile at me, bluer than I remember, with a yearning I recognise.

At Paddington station we delay my departure; another coffee, a later train will do. There is not enough time amongst the departures and arrivals, the rush of people, the station announcer's constant messages, for us two, you and me, to say all we want to.

With reluctance, after three missed trains I have to go. The walk along the platform hurts; I don't want to get on the train and you tell me you don't want me to go. Our hands held, they fit just as well as they always did; our parting embrace stunned us both; without words you opened the train door and we could only look at each other, confused, amazed. Perhaps hopeful.

Lesley Lees

MYSTERY LADY ON THE TRAIN

Are you the lady who was travelling from Birmingham to Torquay on Friday 28th October? We met at Gloucester and travelled on the 11.30am train to Paignton. You left the train at Torre to visit a friend in Torbay Hospital. Would be so good to hear from you.

Yes, actually, that is me. And I could hardly forget you, ever. I have never had an encounter where my heart felt so touched. No, that doesn't do it justice because you touched my soul, and for a week this soul has drifted between heaven and hell. Heaven because I was privileged to spend those hours with you; I've never been so happily delayed. Hell because I'd lost you so quickly; I thought I would never again see the way you wrapped your hand around a cup or smiled a thank you.

By now you should be at home in Cincinnati getting ready to spend Thanksgiving with your daughters. I've read about the extreme weather out there and tried to imagine you shovelling snow from your front porch. But you're still here in Devon? And you're hoping to hear from me? Badly enough to put that ad in the newspaper. I left you my paper that morning; you said you would try to finish my crossword. I laughed and said we spell things differently here; you'll need to use a pencil.

Why aren't you in Cincinnati? Were you searching for me? Strangers on a train. No it's just too clichéd, impossible, why would you, no why ARE you searching for me? No-one else left the train at Torre, no-one but you leant out of the window until it disappeared.

I'll call now.

But where will it lead? Surely there's no point, no future. I can't leave here and you can't leave your girls and the US. No. That was it: a brief moment. I could have bedded you in an instant, but have only the sense - like a sigh - of your hand hovering over my shoulder. I wonder how long I can keep that moment in my mind. For now I feel I will never forget, but we all say that, don't we? Until life gets in the way. I'll still remember at Christmas when I imagine choosing your gift. You told me you're an Aries, so I'll check your horoscope along with mine. By summer I'll think of you less often, and accept that you probably just wanted the name of the book I told you about, a quick lunch before you flew home and that I fooled myself into thinking that you reciprocated.

Besides, what would people think? Silly woman, you can't get involved with strangers. There are some weirdos about. You're so naive. At least it's not as bad as when you pick up hitch-hikers. My friends would all have something to say. *We* have more to say don't we? Where's that number?

Zero . . . seven . . . nine . . . five . . . five . . .

Gilly Goldsworthy

NEIL ARMSTRONG IN
NORTH SOMERSET

It's an unlikely story I'll admit, the first man to walk on the moon turning up at our village pub in North Somerset almost unrecognised twenty years on (this was 1989).

He may have been there for quite a while before anyone noticed, but I guess the price of being the first human to set foot on another world is that someone is bound to recognise you sooner or later, wherever you go. I'm just surprised it was Jim who spotted him.

'Ere Joe, ain't that the bloke what went to the moon? You know the feller, "One small step and all that." Whatsisname?'

'Neil Armstrong?'

'That's the feller, Armstrong.'

'Where?'

'Over there, by the clock. Tall chap. Bald head.'

'Looks a bit like him.'

'It is him, I tell you. Just been in the bog with him. Recognise those feet anywhere.'

'What's he doing here then, Jim?'

'That's what I'd like to know.'

Others seemed less sure.

'Neil who?'

'Armstrong. Neil Armstrong. First man on the moon. One small step and all that.'

'How do you know that's him, Jim?'

'Cause I do. I've seen his picture.'

'What, without his helmet on?'

'Of course.'

'I thought he had to keep his helmet on.'

'Yeh, on the moon, of course, but not down here, yer daft bleeder.'

Naturally, there was an explanation. A man who lived in one of the grander houses worked for the European Space Agency and had arranged a visit by the astronaut as part of a publicity exercise. Unsure how to entertain the great man, his host thought a drop of cider in a quaint village pub might be of interest, which indeed it was. Apparently he consumed several pints of our local brew, a cloudy, greenish liquid guaranteed to give the unsuspecting drinker a restless and sweaty night. I doubt even Neil Armstrong had endured greater discomforts.

So why has this story never been told before? Those feet, here in England's green and pleasant land? Maybe the sparse coverage in the press at the time. A short item did feature in the North

Somerset Gazette, but went largely unnoticed. This may have been because it appeared near the bottom of the inside back page, buried in the sports section, with the ambiguous title:

Moon man barred
as Priory enjoy darts victory

On Friday, regulars of the Half Moon in Shapwick were surprised to find astronaut Neil Armstrong among their number. After an enjoyable evening sampling the local brew, Neil, 52, from Carolina, USA, was invited to take part in a darts match against local rivals, the Priory in Glastonbury. However, following an appeal by the Priory, Mr Armstrong was deemed ineligible under the residency rules of the North Somerset Darts League. The Priory won a closely fought contest 6 – 5.

It may pale by comparison with the front page of Time magazine, but it is still there for all to see on the Gazette website:

www.northsomersetgazette.co.uk/archive/1989

There forever, like that first footprint on the moon.

Richard Bond

One survives, one dies. Now choose.

Derek Thompson

NOT THE MAN I MARRIED

Inspector O'Keefe drove out of his street and into the gridlocked traffic. He looked at his watch. Jeez, 7:50 already. He should be at his desk by now. He would have been, but for his wife.

He drummed his fingers on the wheel and thought about her. Emma's pasty face swam across his consciousness and then bobbed on a gentle swell like a great fat flounder.

He'd grown to hate that face, to despise every wrinkle, every pore, every...

Red, amber, green ...green...GREEN!!!

A cacophony of car horns blasted her face out of the water and triggered O'Keefe into action. He raised a hand in a half-hearted gesture of apology to the car behind and accelerated through the lights.

He rolled his eyes and cursed Emma. She was still causing trouble, even though she was at home in the kitchen sitting on her huge fat backside.

She had a degree in sitting on her arse, a Master's in stuffing her face with crap, and a PhD in moaning.

The moaning recently consisted of her saying that he'd become a different man since he'd joined homicide, that he had no time for her, was obsessed with the job, oh yes, and his favourite – he had become psychologically damaged by his daily immersion in murder.

Stupid melodramatic cow!

O'Keefe chuckled with cold humour and pulled into his parking space. Well, at least when he got home tonight the hole in her face would be silent. Just a lot larger than normal.

The twelve bore had seen to that.

Mandy K. James

PACKING

1. Clothes

Tops: shirts and hoodies

Jeans: ripped, skinny, bootleg

Skirts: mini, maxi, puff

Bras: underwired and padded

Knickers: pretty ones only

Shoes: heels, flats, Converse

2. Makeup (ditch dried-up nail varnish)

3. Jewellery (silver-dip before packing)

4. Hairdryer and straighteners

5. Pencil case

Highlighters

Gel pens

Retractable pencils

6. Ammonite found at Charmouth (wrap in tissue – put in box with flowers on lid)

7. Paperback (any)

8. Pillowcase with Broderie Anglaise trim

9. *Foxy Lady* mug

10. Remember: thermal socks, hot water bottle, Blue Ted, ring binder with campus information

Gail Aldwin

REWARD CHART

She wasn't thinking of him lying in his plastic hospital cot, sucking on his fists. From the window the rooftops had glittered in the January frost; New Year, New Millennium, New Baby.

She thought of none of his milestones: the baby curls, the pearl-sized teeth, his first steps, first bike, the look on his face when he tried on his first football boots.

When they cut him from the mangled car, she could only remember the way he'd pleaded with her not to peel away a sticker, the way his tears had splashed onto his chubby hands as he had tried to prise open her fingers, to release his shiny star.

Josephine Corcoran

THE EARTH MOVED

The work was hard; he had been digging all his life. The rewards were meagre, but enough to sustain his diminutive body. At least he had fulfilled his purpose in life, by producing offspring. They could be anywhere now, also condemned to a life of digging, moving earth.

He heard movement above; a vibration that wasn't natural, fear made him freeze and listen intently.

The spade came down.

Excruciating pain, then nothing.

'Bloody mole has ruined my lawn.'

Rosalind Browne

TRUE COLOURS

I think part of your problem, Steven, is that, on some levels, you don't want to change.'

'That's ridiculous. I have to. People expect me to.'

'Ah ah ah! Now, what did we say about other people's expectations?'

'We don't necessarily have to match them to our own…'

'Exactly. You can be whatever you want to be. Be true to yourself. Forget what anyone else thinks.'

'But doc, that's part of the problem! I can't remember what I was like originally!'

'I'm sorry?'

'It's true! I've spent so long swapping things around that I don't know what I am anymore.'

'Well, what would you like to be?'

'What difference does that make? If I don't change back, my own family won't recognise me, let alone accept me.'

'Nonsense, they'll understand. After all, they're bound to have gone through something similar, don't you think?'

'I guess... Oh, I don't know, this whole thing is too confusing.'

'Don't worry, Steve, I think I might just have a solution.'

'Really? What is it?'

'Relax.'

'That's it?'

'Just try it. That's good... Let all the tension go from your body.'

'This is nice, doc, real nice.'

'Then keep on going. You're almost ready. And… done. Open your eyes.'

'My god, it worked! I'm turning green!'

'In other circumstances, I'd be worried, but, as it's you, I'm delighted. Good to have you back.'

'It's good to be back. Thanks a bunch. I owe you one. See you around, doc.'

'See you around, Steve the Chameleon.'

Brendan Way

ARRIVALS AND DEPARTURES

The passengers of flight BA7098 flood through arrivals, fanning out in a sea of feet and faces, their eyes searching for that special someone on the other side of the barriers. When the stampede has dissipated, the empty expanse in front of me is a reminder of how my life has always been and just why my father and I became estranged.

It's five-forty three in the morning, his connecting flight is late, and already a wave of nausea ripples from my stomach, up through my mouth and across my neck, leaving hot dew that cools clammy cold in its wake. In my haste to leave the house and drive the one hundred miles, I have forgotten the biscuits and now wish that I stopped for that one second to scoop them from the kitchen counter into my bag.

A loud bang echoes from the bowels of the luggage carousel area - I can just about see the conveyor belt if I shift my stance; it reminds me of a game my father and I used to play when I was small - I hear swearing and from left to right, a rotund man passes; pushing a broom behind a collection of drink cartons, crisp packets and other rubbish.

My mouth is dry and I wish I had cleaned my teeth.

I'll give him five more minutes, I think, hoping that this time, when it really matters, he has managed to untangle himself from his seductive mistress and get on the plane.

I stand watching the second hand sweep across my wristwatch dial—the watch was a present from my husband—and as each minute passes the thumping in my ears becomes louder and my throat threatens to throttle me.

The five minutes elapse and the only person to appear, creeping slowly around the corner, is an old man; his sagging jowls covered with salt and pepper stubble, dragging a navy overnight bag behind him.

Time's up, I knew it, he didn't make his flight, I think and fumble for my handkerchief that somehow has escaped its pocket within my handbag. Frustrated, I sigh and resort to wiping my nose on my sleeve.

'You know Mother would disapprove, she'd have told you it wasn't ladylike,' a voice says in a gravelled tone.

He is standing in front of me, his bag at his feet, his arms outstretched, ready to embrace me. A strong smell of acrid perspiration and nauseating cigars hang in the air and instinctively I step backwards.

'What's up Lisa, no kiss for your old Dad?'

'Dad?' I say and again, I take another step backwards.

My eyes scan this abomination of a man in front me, whilst wishing that this longed for reunion wasn't happening in these circumstances. His pale linen suit is creased and the belt of his trousers barely keeps them from sliding over his hips. On his head, a panama hat sits, half-cocked, half hiding the oil slicked white winged hair.

'Well? Aren't you going to ask me how my flight was?' he asks, the furrow on his forehead deepening.

Instead, I ask, 'Who cut your hair?' noting the half-smoked cheroot lodged behind an elephantine ear.

'Just a Chinese barber, I think, in a layover at Helsinki...I can't be sure,' he says, delving into his pockets, looking for his lighter.

'Dad, you can't smoke here,' I say, suppressing my exasperation and need to reproach this shambling mess of a man, who despite his addiction, has flown across three quarters of the world to hold me.

'Oh, can't I? Well, what can I do?' he says, with his hands still in his pockets and a slight trace of saliva escaping from a corner of his mouth.

'For a start,' I say stepping forward, reaching for his half-unbuttoned, blue shirt, 'now that you're finally here, you can let me take care of you.'

When I have finished correcting the straining zigzag mismatch that had exposed patches of belly hair, I straighten his collar and for good measure run my palms down his barrel chest. 'There, that's better,' I say, resisting the urge to hold my nose and swallow hard on the glob of vomit that hit the back of my throat the moment my fingers made contact with him.

'Your Mother used to do that, every time I flew home or before I left her in the departure lounge. I always took it to be a sign of affection,' he says; the corners of his eyes creasing upwards like folds in the curtain-blinds my mother was so fond of. Since she died, I've held back from replacing them with something more contemporary.

'I guess we're good to go then?' he says, offering me the crook of his arm, in order to lead me out of arrivals.

And as we walk through the revolving doors into the cool of a Bristol dawn, with him swaying slightly, I feel his palm brush across my belly and right about now I decide that, despite smelling of tobacco smoke, perspiration and his familiar aftershave blend of cedar wood and cheap wine, my father is still by far the most handsome, debonair man I have ever met. Unlike, the man, who twelve hours earlier, I had watched check in the biggest suitcase he could find; crammed with anything he could lay his hands on, and leave his pregnant wife sobbing in Departures to fly half way across the world to live with a woman he met in a layover in Bangkok.

Natalia Spencer

BOAT TRIP

All night long rain had battered the slate roof and stone walls of the boathouse. Marina pulled on a thick sweater, boots and cagoule and unbolted the door. The wind was gusting even into the sheltered cove where the boathouse stood. She tried to open the solid wooden door, but the wind was too strong. Then, for a moment, the wind slackened. She pushed the door open and slipped out. Just in time, as the wind gathered strength again and hurled the door back into place.

She battled her way down the rough path to the beach, the wind snatching her breath away, rain and salt spray lashing her face. Even the gulls seemed scared, clinging to the cliff face in sullen masses as the gale raged on. The waves were rearing up, pounding the cliffs in fury. *Bucking broncos,* Stefan had said, trying to explain the fury and power of a stormy sea to Marina. *Never go out to sea when the weather is like that.*

Marina trudged back to the boathouse. She was stuck here for another day at least. Still, at least the boathouse was warm and snug. She and Stefan had converted it together into a simple homely cottage for their frequent trips to the coast.

She spent the rest of the day indoors, secure against the elements in the sturdy building of stone and wood. Towards evening she thought the wind was abating and tuned into the shipping forecast. Stefan had taught her how to understand the technical terms and phraseology. She was right: the storm was passing.

The following day the wind had dropped. The sea was calm and a thick quilt of cloud spread across the sky, its greyness mirrored in the dark depths of the sea. Marina could see the Shark's Teeth, the row of granite pillars jutting black and jagged out of the sea just beyond the mouth of the cove, and knew the time had come.

She walked over to the small rowing boat in which she and Stefan used to fish in the cove. Stowing her bag with care in the stern, she dragged the boat into the water and jumped in. She pulled steadily out to sea, drawing comfort from the rhythmic motion of the oars. Drawing level with the Shark's Teeth, she shipped her oars and for a few moments sat still as the boat bobbed up and down. Above her head the gulls swooped and sailed on the unseen air currents with insolent ease.

Marina took the urn out of her bag and to the threnody of the gulls' mocking calls, scattered the ashes it contained onto the sea. Stefan was in the place he loved best.

As Marina rowed back to land the mist rolled in behind her. She beached the boat and looked back out to sea. There was nothing to see but fog.

Iris Lewis

CITY OF GOLD

Yesterday was a very bad day. Today I'm better. I'm always better when I'm outside. Perhaps it's the open space; perhaps it's just that I'm not stuck in the flat running round after George.

I walk along the towpath. One or two boats moving along the canal, a few moored on this side. One is new looking, fresh paint, dark green with a cream roof and the name picked out in gold: "Egoli". Funny name. Wonder what it means?

If George and I had a boat, what would be a good name for it?

Cooped up in a narrowboat, I'd call it "Hell on Earth"… Always assuming I could get him on board.

I shouldn't be thinking like this. He couldn't help getting MS and ending up in a wheelchair, but his temper's getting worse along with the disability.

My one-day-a-week respite becomes a beacon of hope - the light at the end of a very dark tunnel. Today, I'm breaking free. I'm getting on this boat, undoing the rope and chugging off into the distance, into the country, through locks and bridges and stopping at a waterside pub for dinner and a glass of wine. I find myself standing on the deck, my hand on the tiller, the shining brass finial silky smooth under my fingers.

'Can I help you?'

A man emerges from below and looks at me in surprise. Snowy-haired, deeply tanned and a pleasant smile.

'I'm so sorry.'

I'm struggling to find an explanation for my invasion of his territory

'I was admiring your boat and I wonder what the name "Egoli" means?'

He looks out across the water. 'I've worked in Africa most of my life. I always dreamed I'd buy a boat when I retired and just meander along the waterways. "Egoli" is African. It means City of Gold. Everyone needs a city of gold to dream of, don't you agree?'

He looks at me, his expression kind and understanding, and I get the feeling he knows all about me.

'Yes, yes,' I agree. 'Thank you. Goodbye.'

I climb onto the towpath and walk slowly back to the road. I'll go and get a nice bottle of wine to have with our dinner tonight. Perhaps I can find my own city of gold if I try hard enough. Perhaps George and I can find one together. I smile to myself and turn towards home.

Hazel Bagley

HARNESS

Three little sisters played happily in the street. No fear of enemy planes this sunny day, the second year of the war. Annie held the reins, in which toddler Meg was firmly strapped. Tiny Meg enjoyed trotting forward whenever Vera and Annie said 'Gee-up Dobbin,' just like the rag-and-bone man did. Occasionally the older sisters, no older than four and five, tied the reins to the silver lamp post. They were imitating the regular carthorse drivers stopping on their rounds. Suddenly an air raid siren sounded. Annie and Vera panicked, rushing into the house for safety.

Grandma was horrified when a worried neighbour delivered a sobbing Meg. Mummy was furious. Sent upstairs, to await the inevitable punishment when Father returned, neither Annie nor Vera could understand why the adults were so angry. Didn't they understand it was only a game?

Margaret Bradshaw

I TOLD YOU SO

'I told you, Mummy, I can't do it. People will laugh!'

'No they won't,' I say.

'The words will lump in my throat and won't come out.' Joe stamps his small foot.

'It's nothing to get emotional about. Pretend only Daddy and I are watching.'

Joe sulks. 'All right. If you *promise* no-one will laugh.'

'I *promise.*'

I'm in the fourth row back. The curtains open, and emotion lumps in my throat. I swallow hard to hold it in.

Joseph, red-chequered teacloth on his head, stands centre-stage, bravely pushing words from his mouth … and a finger up his nose.

Deborah Rickard

TRAPPED IN NOMANSLAND

The air in the house has become stale and still. Things keep going missing and they are pointing the blame my way. I didn't take any trinket, I have more interesting things to touch and claim: growing things, temporal shifting things that would fade if they were stolen.

I sit in my garden, hugging my legs, and I look at these beautiful fragile things: orange and pink and green and gilded burgundy. My knees are bare and white with pin-prick goosebumps. Smells of wood smoke and earth reach my button nose. I push myself to my feet and gaze towards the woods. The field slopes towards the forest fringe and mist hangs there, drifting like a newly-dead ghost.

My feet crunch the leaves on my way down the garden towards the field. The blackberry thorns snag my skirt as I push the gate open. It sits skewed and won't close properly. I glance back at the house standing tall and grey, fading wisteria clinging to the masonry, and then I turn towards the forest and start walking. I can hear the horn of a hunt. It echoes like a bruise on the land.

The hedgerows are ripe and the wheat is long-harvested; the field is stubbly and barren brown. It sticks to my boots.

Soon I am in the mist. The forest is close. I curl my fingers into the sleeves of my duffel coat and bury my chin in the collar. The path carves between leaning ash and beech; the woodland floor is crisp with dead leaves and the skeletons of bluebells and stitchwort.

Some way along the path I spot a shimmer. At first I think it's a smooth pebble catching the light. But when I draw nearer I see that it is misshapen and not at all stone-like. I kneel down on the path and feel the damp earth impress through the dry leaves against my skin. It's a gold cork-stopper: one of the missing items from the house. I pick it up. It is heavy and cold. I look around but there's no one here, everything's quiet. I don't dare to slip it into my pocket, so I keep clutching it and walk on. Next I see a gold ring glinting like a winking eye to the side of the pathway where animal tracks lead deeper into the woods. I follow the track until I come to a fox den. It smells here. I'm about to turn and leave when I spot the glistening of a silver chain. It snakes into the foxhole. I step closer, and then even closer.

There are more of the missing treasures scattered here.

I wonder what a fox could possibly want from all this gold and silver? Then I hear the horn again, haunting brass tone distorted through fog and twisting branches. It sounds jovial and mocking. I stand here in nomansland clutching cold metal, sitting like a duck between two sides of an ancient war.

Many paws pad on sticky mud. Hooves churn the path and leave small circular puddles. I drop the cork-stopper and ring into the foxhole and set off running through the forest. Branches slap my face and scratch perforated red trails on my arms. The wind rushes. I can hear paw pads and thumping hooves, sometimes close and sometimes far. It feels as if I will be running forever. The forest envelopes me and I no longer know which way I'm running. Soon I forget why I am running. All I know is that if I stop I will be swallowed up whole; perhaps I am already swallowed.

Jennifer Bell

PAINTING THE SHED

I hear the first scream while I am painting the shed, kneeling in my brother's old school shorts on a pile of yellowed newspapers.

'No! She's not dead!'

Great Uncle Jazeps, known to me as Uncle Jaz, gave me the timber shack today. It leans towards the fence, and one of the boards has slipped, leaving a triangle of sunlight on the back wall. He also let me have all the old tins of paint and second-hand brushes on the shelves.

'You paint, make pretty, huh? *Ya*?' Uncle Jaz had offered. 'Maybe Auntie Pauline will give you mat for floor?'

'*Ya*, Uncle Jaz.' It was almost the only Latvian word I knew, along with "Soodi", which I knew meant "shit". I wasn't allowed to say "shit" but "Soodi" was all right. I watched him lever the lid off with an old chisel, turquoise paint flaking onto the floor in bright flecks.

Great Aunt Pauline often shouts, but the shrieks sound different now. I scoot forward to look out of the door.

As she bellows, Auntie Pauline folds in the middle, until she runs out of sound, thin curls hanging down. Then she unfolds, the air squeezing back into her with a wail, like a pair of nylon, floral bellows. Uncle Jaz pats her as she rises, shaking his head. All I can pick out is the word 'Jimmy.'

I hope he's not coming home, to take his old room back.

I dip the most pliable brush into the paint. It's the colour of the bathroom wall, where it clashes with the primrose bath, sink and toilet. Where Uncle Jaz goes every morning with the Angling Times. At some point he sings some of the Latvian anthem, partly in Russian because he learned it at school. The first brushful glows against the faded creosote.

Words float through the missing window pane.

'That T'resa, she was never good enough for our Jimmy.' Hiccoughs punctuate Auntie Pauline's shrill voice.

I like Teresa, she gives me sweets when she babysits: sherbet lemons that fountain sharpness and sugar into my mouth; butterscotch blocks in silver paper.

'Is accident. It must be accident.' Uncle Jaz, stretching the English words into funny shapes, shaking his head, white hair flowing onto his collar, blue eyes lost in nests of wrinkles.

The turquoise covers five long boards and starts the sixth. It rolls off the edges where creosote has oozed in from outside, forming balls of glossy colour. The next pot is called 'Autumn Peach' and is the colour of the best back room, the one reserved for guests. It has twin beds and matching polyester bedspreads that slide off the second you sit on them. The paint smells like new plasters, and is a similar shade. It's thin at the top, solid at the bottom. It runs down the boards and streaks the floor.

The neighbour's in the garden too, the one Auntie Pauline calls "that fat slut." She's soothing, I can hear lots of "loveys" and "pets".

'I know he never done it, Cath.'

Cath's voice doesn't quite penetrate the shed, so I stand on one of the other tins to look through the dust and spiders' webs on the window.

'It must have been an accident. Don't you worry, pet. It will all get sorted out.'

'The police have always had it in for my boy.' Pauline starts wailing again. The police are always arresting Jimmy. He seems to spend every winter in HMP Portsmouth.

When I look back at my work, the end wall of the shed is now more gravy-coloured than Autumn Peach, so I try another tin. It's bright pink, and covered in a thick layer of khaki oil. I stir it a bit with the screwdriver. I pick a slat at random and touch the brush to it, paint oozing down the bristles and dropping a lazy 'S' and a few spheres of colour into the dust of the floor.

Uncle Jaz is shouting now. 'Pauline!' Then a lot of words, some Latvian, some words I'm not allowed to say. I peer around the door to see two policemen holding his arms. He's crying, great sobs barking around the garden.

'Is good lad, means no harm...' He keeps lapsing into Latvian, which only Auntie Pauline can understand. Everyone is shouting.

'My boy wouldn't hurt a fly!'

'There's a young woman dead, Mrs Balodis. Someone knocked her down.'

The other neighbours hiss and growl like cats, standing by the shed.

'I hear he ran her over with her own car.' Mrs Madderly, whose husband always wanted us to reach into his trouser pocket for a toffee.

'I hear he reversed over her.' Mrs Pruitt, who told my brother off for falling off her wall and breaking his arm. 'That Jimmy was always trouble. His mother is a bag of nerves.'

'Poor Teresa. She was such a sweet girl. Not too bright, though, hanging out with Jimmy.'

The inch of blue in the battered tin is thick, the brush trampolining on the skin until I stir it a bit. I wipe it off on the corner of some newspaper. It goes on like blue cheese spread, and smells similar.

Mrs Pruitt has to speak louder over the commotion. 'They're a bad family, I've always said it.' Mrs Pruitt, who Uncle Jaz took to the hospital when her husband has his veins done. 'And those kids, in and out of care.'

I slide back into the shed, crouch over the tins and brushes with their broken promises. I will go back to the children's home. Pea-green walls and urine flavoured mattresses. My eyes start to itch with tears, and I rub my sleeve over my face, leaving a smear of wetness from the paint. It might be for Teresa, but it's probably for me.

Rebecca Alexander

LOP

She pointed to the tree with her good hand and smiled politely when the tree surgeon asked her why she hadn't called him in the first place.

Rachel Carter

POLISHING THE AIR

West London, traffic lights at red. On National
Express 035 coach, sitting high up near the back,
with a good view over the stopped traffic. My
eyes light on floor-to-ceiling glass, the length of a
first floor. And a person behind it, waving, arms at
full stretch. Holding something. No, I think, not
waving, and into my mind floats (or better sinks)
but drowning. But that's silly, it's not that. He's
polishing, polishing the glass which is already so
clear, so unfingerprinted, so unreflecting of the
low winter sun that even its transparency isn't real,
and he seems to be polishing the air and might fall

over the edge with too vigorous a movement or a single forward step. Yes, he's polishing the air.

And suddenly we're in conversation, the polisher and me.

'Yes, that's what I'm doing,' he says, not stopping, 'that's what I do. Once it's all clean and shiny inside, I polish the air and make it shiny too. Not everyone sees that, but you did.' He puts his head on one side and eyes me. 'And I moonlight, sometimes.'

Moonlight, cool, clear and silvery, is just right, I think and almost say.

But he's going on. 'I can make you shiny too, if you like.'

'Sorry?' He couldn't have said what I thought, surely.

'Yeah, shiny.' He pauses, and makes a contemplative sweep high up with his left hand.

'Shiny,' I say flatly.

'Look as though you could do with a bit of the old shine in your life, you do.'

What is this – a pickup? Am I dealing with a madman, or a magician maybe?

'I know what you're thinking – ' (actually he seems to be doing just that, sensing the prickle of fear in me) ' – and listen, it's all right, love, honest.' (*Love*?) He goes on patiently. 'I just put a bit of shine in people's lives. Look at her, now. Wanted to float, she did, and there she goes.'

He leans forward and points downwards to the pavement, polishing cloth still in his hand, and through the ankle-deep London plane leaves walks a young lady, floating as he says. Her narrow pale jeans just melt into the leaves, no shoes, no feet. But – I see it all now – yes, boots, the exact same biscuit colour as the fallen leaves, very strange.

'You did that, the leaves, the boots?'

'Yeah. Well, a bit funny when you think about it, but it was what she wanted,' he says defensively. And what *he* wanted was something to cuddle.' This time he waves his cloth like a flag, beckoning towards the corner at the end of the building. On cue, like an actor waiting in the wings, walks a bearded guy with long hair. He carries a guitar, no case, strung over his shoulder with a woven band. I feel for the right word, *hippy,* and then, seeing his relaxed smile, *happy hippy.* I almost expect him to greet me with *Love* or *Peace.* Nestled in the fold of his arms is a placid marmalade cat, same colour as the leaves – it might disappear if it walked on the pavement. Round the cat's neck is a knitted patterned scarf.

'Hey, man,' shouts the cleaner. The hippy's hands are full, so all he can do is toss his head in reply. I can't decide if they know each other or not, but by now I'm not sure of anything much.

'You mean you gave –'

'Fixed it for him, bit of shine. Kittens? NO problem. Now heads,' he drops his hands to his sides, 'heads and hearts, they need a bit more shine, wouldn't you say? So back to you. You would like to be shiny, wouldn't you? I see it in your eyes. He used to have sad eyes like yours, and look at him now.'

Shiny? Me? Not what I want, really not what I want. He's taking over. How am I going to get out of this?

'You'll be OK. Come on up here,' he says hospitably, 'beside me,' and stretches a hand through the glass, through it like liquid. And abruptly, and as surprisingly as we had fallen into conversation I'm through the glass and by his side, one floor up. He smiles.

'Just a little bit of shine, as it's your first time, right?'

He is a magician, no doubt about it. I do feel better, no longer the dull matt person I'd been since the events of the previous year. I've moved on, moved on even from where I was a few minutes ago.

The lights turn green, and the bus swings round the roundabout, bucketing on a rough piece of road.

'Thanks,' I send in his direction, 'for the shine.'

He's polishing again. Or waving. I seem to hear him say, 'You'll be able to do it for yourself the next time.'

Yes. And I say aloud, 'yes, I believe I can.'

Muriel Higgins

THE ALIEN'S UNFORTUNATE TIMING

Fat Bob was chomping one of his special meat pies when the alien landed.

His doorbell rang.

'Greetings,' said the alien. 'Are you the leader?'

'Huh?' said Fat Bob through gravy and crumbs. He looked down at the visitor. 'Hey this ain't Hallowe'en already is it?' He hated the whole thing. Last year he had opted for 'trick'. No way was he parting with one of his beloved pies. They had lured him out into the garden onto a patch of autumn leaves. But the leaves gave way. The devils had dug a pit and it was two days before he got out.

He wiped a greasy sleeve across his mouth. He really wanted to get back to his pie and chips. And a second pie, chicken surprise, was warming in the oven. The oven Martha had got at the dump. Resourceful Martha. The door kept falling off and one ring worked only if two of the others were on. We're wasting gas he would say timidly. But she insisted her innumerable 'bargains' outweighed the utility bills. His trousers fitted her better. He was used to being led, and anyway she was one hell of a pie-maker. But as he got fatter she got thinner. Rare wasting disease the doctor had said. Then one day she wasn't there anymore. He sure missed her pies. He experimented and pretty soon had the hang of it. And he could be resourceful too. He found breeding and slaughtering his own chickens cost-effective. Then he discovered roadkill, and was not averse to adding snails, beetles and suchlike.

He grinned at the bug-like creature on the doorstep. He'd give it trick or treat.

'I guess I am the leader. Good first question,' Fat Bob said. 'Hey, good disguise too. Come right on in.'

Michael Kirby

THE TOLL OF BLUE SKY
THINKING

The bright March sky was a flat reprimand. Sylvia avoided meeting it. Straightening her rigid net curtains, she glanced sideways at the day's nagging blueness. Thick and opaque, weighted with a strip of lead, the nets cramped the light, keeping it like folded ice. She moved to the kitchen and slanted the blind against the sun's reaching fingers. She would not be lured out.

There had been safety in winter gloom. The chill, damp months had been her friend; had given her excuses aplenty. Her heart did not want to be woken. Darkness was a numbness she had got used to. Daffodils disturbed her. They glared their yellowness, trumpeting change. Time was moving in the wrong direction. She wanted the past again; the self she used to be.

The armchair was an embrace. Slumped, head down against the future, Sylvia longed for the years that had given her the best of her life. The date-arrested calendar above her head was holding back the worst of times, but the days kept on bringing them anyway.

Molly pushed the handwritten note through the letterbox: muted lilac paper, a picture of violets (somehow soothing) her carefully chosen words below in blue ink - an invitation to tea. Should she really be writing an invitation to something like tea? What did other people do? It felt, in this case, like the right thing. A cautious move; not too sudden. Face to face might be too much.

Molly pictured herself laying the tea table, gracing it with her grandmother's white lace tablecloth, her mother's rose-patterned tea service, each an inheritance she didn't deserve. She imagined her own hands fulfilling the gestures performed for her countless times by hands aged and worn. Her assertions across the tea table had pushed her cup towards them, daring them to fill it with something new, something impossible. Breaking brittle biscuits, she had sipped tea with a sense that communion was pointless. Her terms had been strict. They had failed to apply to anyone except herself alone…

Molly had only fully glimpsed her neighbour once in the short time since moving to this street. Molly had knocked on the door, wishing to borrow milk. She had noticed that her neighbour had deliveries from the milkman. Everything seemed to be delivered to the door – groceries, parcels… invitations to tea. The door didn't deliver to the world. The world came knocking.

When Molly had knocked, it had opened on a sad-faced woman, her expression somehow a darkening of the shadows in her hallway. In that grainy interior, loneliness had grown into a beast that prowled the threshold. The woman held it back by the collar, her eyes turned down in self-conscious defeat.

Ever since that moment, the woman – Sylvia – had preyed on Molly's mind, mixing with memories of her mother, her grandmother, the ways in which Molly had, over and over, let them down. She did not like to contemplate her past, or the person she used to be. It had been the worst of times. But it was behind her now. The daffodils in Sylvia's garden were like sentinels to the future. Molly would make amends. Not to her mother, not to her grandmother - not directly anyway. Her regrets gathered round the fact that it was too late for that now. But she could change - move forward.

As she posted the invitation through the letterbox, pulled her fingers from its spring, Molly thought of the poet John Donne. She pictured him in the old St Paul's, its stone-cold space swimming with the multi-faceted gleams and shadows of diverse minds. She imagined them gathered together in a net of words by the poet dean, whose journey through the passionate life had washed him to a shore where 'No man is an island.'

No woman neither.

Returning to her kitchen, Molly wrote in the date a few days ahead on her calendar – 'Tea - with Sylvia.' She would keep on knocking.

'Never send to know for whom the bell tolls,' she said to herself, resolute, flicking the calendar to look ahead at the months that would be her change.

'It tolls for thee.'

Melanie Doherty

A WARTIME SECRET

'It was bone-chillingly cold, snow was sifting down from the sky. Through the blizzard I caught fleeting glimpses of light. I stumbled towards it. Eventually I made out the shape of a building, ghost-grey through the snow. Shelter, I thought. As I drew nearer I could see it was a cottage, light shining from its windows, smoke pluming from the chimney.

I tried to run, but could only slip and slide towards it. At last I reached the cottage and banged on the door. No answer. I hammered on it again and again, desperation lending me strength.

At last the door opened. Beyond it stood a woman. As soon as she saw me, she tried to slam the door shut, but I was too quick. I forced my way in.

The woman stood and stared at me, a look of dawning horror on her face. For a few moments we held each other's gaze without speaking. At last I found my voice. "Food, shelter," I said, in halting Polish. Beyond her I could see the kitchen. A fire smouldered in the hearth, above it hung a cooking pot, gently steaming.

I pushed past the woman into the kitchen. She followed me in. I stripped off my sodden overcoat and pulled off my boots. I gestured to the woman to take them. It was only then she started to speak, first in Polish and then, when it was clear that I was only able to pick up a word or two, in broken German.

I was ravenous and pointed to the stew bubbling gently over the fire. She ladled some out into a bowl. I devoured it. It was thin, more like gruel than soup, but blessedly hot. I felt warmth seeping through my body. I asked for more. She poured the last of the stew into my bowl. There was none left for her, but I didn't care about that.

Darkness soon fell. We passed the evening together. She told me her name was Marya, her husband had died a few months earlier and she was trying to keep their smallholding going. In a strange way it was companionable. What happened next seemed only natural. I pulled her into my arms. She was thin, her shoulders bony. She didn't resist, she was too fragile, too frightened. I pushed her onto the floor and pressed down on her. She didn't struggle or cry out. It was soon over.

By morning it had stopped snowing and the air was clear. In the weak sunshine I was able to get my bearings. I hadn't strayed far from my platoon. I could soon be with them again. I pulled on my boots and overcoat and left.'

Jack paused and looked at the girl sitting on the other side of the fireplace. For a few moments all that could be heard was the ticking of the clock on the mantelpiece.

At last the girl spoke. 'Father Kaminski says you were captured and held prisoner of war by the British.'

'Yes. I was held in the North of England. A couple of years after the war the prisoners in my camp were released. Many returned to Germany, but I had nothing to return to. I wanted to make a fresh start, put the past behind me. I stayed in England, changed my name to Jack Smith, found work. Gradually I was accepted into the community, but could never really settle, even after ten years. I kept thinking of Marya and what I'd done to her. In the end I had to come back and try to make amends. I found the nearest village to the cottage, asked for the local priest, told him everything and asked him to help me find Marya. For some reason I never thought she could have died. I still saw her as I remembered her, young, slender, delicate.'

The girl looked straight at him, but said nothing. The silence yawned like a chasm between them. At last she spoke, her words tumbling out of her in a rush. 'My mother died when I was a baby. People say it's because she was weak from near starvation, but I think she died of shame. She wouldn't tell anyone who my father was. Father Kaminski found an elderly couple in the village to bring me up. I've always wondered who my father was.'

'And now you know.' Jack looked at the girl, sitting upright in her chair opposite him. She looked innocent, vulnerable. He ached with love for her.

'Yes,' she said, 'now I know.'

Iris Lewis

BEST SERVED COLD

They may have looked pretty, but the yellow suede pumps – bought especially for the trip – hid two sizeable blisters and enough dead skin cells to create a small artificial beach. Jenny was dying to slip them off, but she suspected they would smell like a school locker room.

The Moroccan sun glared down, a burning copper penny in the sky. She closed her eyes, leaning back against the whitewashed wall, trying to ignore the unsettled stirrings of last night's lamb.

When a shadow fell across her she sighed with relief.

It was short-lived.

'Miss Williams! Are you going to find out where our tea is? It's eleven o'clock!'

Jenny looked up into a fat, sweaty face that made her fingers twitch into a fist.

'Certainly, Mrs Walton-Clarke,' she said, summoning a smile. 'I'll just see to it.'

As soon as they were in the car the shoes were coming off.

Rin Simpson

LUCKY PANTS

'Good morning, sir. Can I help?'

'I wish to buy lucky pants. Girl I chat in bar yesterday say "no" when I ask... you know. She laugh and say Dmitri not wearing lucky pants. I did not know. Is shame, very shame.'

Tina pepped her professional smile. Dmitri's accent suggested his handicap was idiom, not idiocy. Idiom and optimism.

'Men's underwear is second floor.'

'Yes. Man there say ask you.'

Darren. Bloody Darren. Bloody childish. Anything he could do to wind her up. He still couldn't accept she'd turned him down. Her smile straightened out, paused a moment in thought... and revived, a little sharper, a little less professional.

'Could you take these and show them to him?'

She took a pair of knickers down from the display and wrote on them: 'Mmm, thanks, Dmitri. I got lucky. Love, Tina.'

Kevlin Henney

IVORY TOWERS

On the planet Ibis, covered in turquoise ocean, a young warrior stood on a white beach looking to the sky tinged green and the harsh binary stars. The warrior's name was Malock, and, like all large life on Ibis, they were a multitude of life - not just a single entity. A consensus of organisms held together by flimsy filaments so they could cooperate. Malock thought as a hive, but a hive that moved on two apparent legs, a hive that was contained in a single form. Malock was a colony, but mobile; not fixed as rock. It was a trick their ancestors had learnt in the seas, as they left the reef bed.   Specialisation of specific members allowed so much, and Malock's form thought they were the peak of the evolutionary ladder.

They were wrong.

Malock picked up a crude spear that they had made out of a dead leaf colony. Such colonies built their structures from a hard fibrous substance and the creatures on the edge became specialised light collectors to help feed the rest. Leaf colonies could be huge: the one Malock held was about the same height as Malock and thinner than their apparent wrist.   They had been entrusted with a sacred mission. Sighing deeply, they thought in unison about the task ahead and ran into the sea. Their apparent feet, flat and flipper-like, kicked up the fine white sand made from reef-colony secretions.

Malock opened their eyes; the world shimmered and rippled, distances were no longer the same. A lensing film flopped in front of their light receptor specialists and they swam, powerfully and strongly. Their lungs shut down and an older form of respiration began, slits allowing the warm rich water to enter into the mist of the colony. The founder members still remembered incarnations when they had not left the sea's warm languidness.

They swam out into the darker waters, deeper and cooler. Currents swirled, threatening to drag them in an unchosen direction. They gritted their apparent teeth and swam resolutely onwards. Floating colonies made clouds in which Malock had to wade. The reefs made the founders hum with an ancient homesickness. They left the glittering world behind, heading for the deeps. They altered their internal pressure and went deeper.

Predator colonies swam here, whose faded colours and sleek forms made them hard to detect. Malock had to be aware of every ripple. The light was dim and they had to shift to a different type of vision, which made the world into a grainy, luminous, monotone. But the deeps were no stranger to their colony-form. They had offered protection from the periodic solar blasts that had scoured the planet's surface through the ages. The founders gave Malock and others of their form a genetic memory, each creature within a colony able to lock itself away, separate and be born anew, memories intact but jumbled.

Something in one of the Founders had ignited such a memory: they were heading for something, something important. Malock swam through the fire of fatigue. Some of the creatures died of toxins or lack of oxygen, others were so old the effort obliterated them, but still Malock swam, swam down deep and deeper. The creatures of the colony slept in fits and starts so that 60 percent were always functioning as they plunged onward. They swam until even the grainy light went and direction seemed meaningless, and yet they swam onwards until from the abyss a faint star appeared in the blackest of nights. It grew stronger and another appeared, followed by two more and then suddenly the world was full of starlight.

The stars coalesced to form a myriad paratopia of small creatures, single and on their own. Occasionally bundles of entangled organisms would form. They glowed with their own light. Malock watched in wonder as one budded a small replica of itself. This was the cradle. Malock could feel the warmth. The water bubbled mineral rich, it had a soapy feel. Malock swam on, fear tingeing their collective thoughts. The heat was becoming unbearable and more of them died. The colony knew the danger of this: they were becoming stupid. Each creature's death, regardless of how permanent, made them thicker. Thinking was getting harder and yet they were driven on towards the warmth, the ruddy light ahead.

White towers of scalding bubbles poured rich life-giving smoke into the sea. 'The Ivory Towers,' the founders whispered. And Malock knew they were almost there, but Malock was disintegrating. They had failed, they would die and their mission with them... what had it been again?

Find the origin? Find the safety of the Nursery? Those things made no sense now. Malock wondered why they had left the cities built as mocking effigies of the reefs. Surely they had been safe?

Welcome Malock a voice glittered in the water.

Malock shuddered. 'Who?' they wondered sluggishly.

We are everything reverberated around the disintegrating colony.

'Everything?' managed the remnants of Malock.

Yes everything. We have been waiting for you.

'But we are dying. We were supposed to save... something?'

You have. You have brought yourselves here to the crucible. Others will follow but may have left it too late. Your... elements will be the new world. You will lie dormant until the cleansing of stars is passed, then each fragment of you will be a new life. You are the new founders.

'But the cities... ?'

They will live again through you and others of your form, they are... the next level, next time they will become.

'Become?'

The cities will live and then... then we can truly be once more.

'?'

The cities will reform us, and we will truly think once more. We have been dormant for so long, thinking the thoughts of the small.

Malock could no longer answer as awareness drifted apart and floated to the hot mineral sands below.

The World sighed and went back to waiting.

Sarah Snell-Pym

LATE NIGHT FICTION

'Just another couple of pages,' he promised, as the clock chimed one. A gulp of stewed tea the only reward for perseverance.

'Half a page more, then sleep,' he whispered, as the clock struck two.

But at three o'clock he dropped his pen, weary of the writer's art, and yielded to the morning.

The tax form would have to wait.

Derek Thompson

BAPTISM OF FIRE

October 1st. Ruth's baptism day. A chapel packed with friends, relatives and the plain curious. Only the front pew was empty. It was solid, sturdy, larger and grander than the others, its arms finished off with a daring scroll, a testament in wood to the authority of the chapel elders of old. Ruth sat in the row behind, innocent, ethereal in the loose white robes draping her slight girlish figure. Behind her a bobbing of heads, a shuffling of bottoms, a moving patchwork of colours as the individual worshippers melded into one congregation. A comforting quilt of sound -

clacking heels, *great honour, lovely girl,* throaty chuckles, *visiting preacher, famous you know.* Ruth sat in quiet contemplation as the hubbub went on around her.

'He's here.' A Chinese whisper passed up and down the pews. A Mexican wave of craning necks, as the welcoming party led by the Reverend William Walker (Billy to the congregation) ushered the guest to the front. The deacons filed into their seats, the baptism pool in front of them.

Billy spoke first, his lullaby-lilting voice unusually hoarse and hesitant as he welcomed the famous evangelist and invited him to address the congregation and conduct the baptism. As he bowed his head in prayer the rays of the autumn sun pierced the windows high above the gallery, illuminating his sweating bald head like a beacon. A light to lighten the gentiles, thought Ruth with a hastily suppressed giggle.

Introduction over, Billy settled his comfortably padded bottom into the large oak minister's chair, his normally twinkling eyes cast down and smiling, chubby face composed into solemnity. The congregation sat still and the hush deepened. All eyes were drawn, like iron filings to a magnet, to the gaunt figure at the front. He sat there in cadaver-like stillness, his face unmoving, his petrol-blue eyes piercing through everyone, yet looking at no one.

The silence continued. Ruth felt the tension twisting inside her like a tourniquet. She was as taut as a spring. Just when she thought she could bear the strain no longer, the pastor rose and strode to the lectern. As he preached Old Testament certainties and New Testament salvation the sun's rays played on his head. His dense mass of ginger curls was transformed into a burning bush. His voice crackled with the flames of hell. His face glowed with Pentecostal zeal. There was no room in his Father's House for fragile, faith-doubting humanity. As she listened to him Ruth could hear the screams of heretics dragged to the stake.

It was time to receive Ruth into the faith. The Reverend took off his shoes and socks, rolled up his trouser legs and stepped into the pool. He waded to the middle and stood there, tall, upright, motionless, a granite pillar of faith. Ruth looked about her, confused. What was she to do? She couldn't go through with it. She was scared. Scared of the preacher, frightened of the water, terrified of the hell-fire that surely would consume her if she did nothing. She sat quite still, riven with fear and indecision.

'Come on, dear, it's time.' Mrs Walker was next to her, coaxing her onto her feet and guiding her towards the pool. Ruth stepped with elfin grace into the baptistery. She knelt down in the water at the preacher's feet and bowed her head as he said a prayer. She sat down in the pool and the preacher bent over her, his face so near she could almost smell the smoke of burning heretics on his breath, see the flames of hell ignited by those staring petrol eyes. He pushed her back and held her down until feet, legs, hips, breasts, arms, head, face were totally immersed. Ruth's white gown billowed up like a balloon as if to waft her into heaven in a state of grace, her sins washed away.

With one theatrical gesture the pastor pulled her to her feet and left her to cough and splutter her way out of the pool. The congregation erupted into applause. Mrs Walker was waiting, holding out a big, fluffy white towel. She wrapped Ruth in it.

'Welcome,' she whispered. 'Welcome into the fold.'

The preacher was still in the pool, speaking in tongues. He stopped. The congregation sat watchful, expectant. For a moment he stood, statue-like, his eyes cinder-dark as though in a trance. He threw up his arms and shouted, 'Alleluia, praise the Lord!'

As one, the congregation leapt to its feet and shouted in spontaneous unison, 'Alleluia, praise the Lord!'

Billy looked at Ruth, looking like a woolly lamb in her towel, caught her eye and winked. Tension flowed out of her, leaving her cool, composed, refreshed.

It was done, she thought, she was baptised, born again.

Iris Lewis

KISSING FRANKENSTEIN

On her hundred and first birthday she said,

'I was the first actor to speak in a talkie, you know,'

and,

'Boris Karloff, what a sweet man.'

'I want a dog,' said her great-granddaughter, crouched at her feet, demolishing a cupcake. But the old woman was dreaming of movie sets, she only 19, Karloff already a star.

Later, after the cupcakes had gone, along with cousins neither the old lady nor her great-granddaughter knew, she was taken back to her room.

'Boris Karloff,' she murmured, wondering what old age really meant. Would she have allowed that kiss while the crew were taking down the set if she'd known that, eighty-two years later – oh my! - she would be the only one remembering?

'Why ever not?' she declared. 'He had the softest lips!'

'Whose lips are soft?' demanded the child. The old lady's son just grinned.

'Boris Karloff, Mum?' he said, taking her hand. 'You and Frankenstein?'

'I shan't tell!' said the old lady. 'He swore me to secrecy. He was married, you know.' She turned to the child. 'They rise from their graves,' she said, eyes wide. 'And then they eat you!'

The little girl didn't even blink. She climbed on the bed.

'I love your face,' she said, stroking her great-grandmother's cheek.

'You minx,' said the birthday girl, recognising something that she would leave behind, something that would carry on without her.

Tania Hershman

THE BOWER BIRD AND THE
BUTTERFLY CHARMER

The air is warm, for the first time this year. The sun is shining. He pauses and she realises he has led her to the kitchen shop. Like a bower bird outside his construction, he stands at the door and shyly entices her in. She hesitates on the threshold, not unwillingly, but as if registering that at this moment, on this threshold, something significant, something enormous, is at stake. As the automatic door slides open he leads her into a brightly lit vastness, a treasure cave behind the modest façade.

They pause beside the pretty little gadgets. The bean-slicer, the melon-corer, best of all the strawberry-stalk-remover.

'We could have strawberries,' he says. 'In summer. On picnics.'

She points to the small mini-mixer in its transparent plastic pot. 'We could make whipped cream, too.'

A sales consultant approaches them, avid, unctuous. 'Do you need any help there?'

Not the kind of help you can give me, he thinks.

Only if you could make him say it, she thinks.

They pass by shelves stacked and decked and hung with bakeware: bread tins, cake tins, sandwich tins, madeleine tins, muffin tins, whoopee pie tins, in grey metal and bright silicone.

'I wish I could bake. I never went to cookery lessons,' she says sorrowfully. 'Can't even boil an egg.'

He points to an array of silicone pods, in a choice of colours. 'We could use those,' he says.

'It says they are egg poachers,' she says. 'Not the same thing.' But she is pleased at what he seems to be suggesting.

'They have special little gadgets to lift them out of the boiling water,' he says. 'That's a safety feature.'

She smiles at him. 'You won't scald your fingers.'

He is giving her safety. He cares.

The shop funnels them further in, enticing them towards more and greater opportunities in its bright depths.

'You like eggs, don't you?' he asks.

'Love them!' she says. *Would she say that about anything he might mention?*

He points to the electric omelette-maker.

'We wouldn't even need a cooker,' he says, 'Not with one of these.'

Is he thinking what she thinks he's thinking?

'Look, there's a cupcake-maker,' she says, urging him to say more.

'And there's a soup machine.' He reads the label: ' "Chops, boils, simmers, blends…" This is the life.'

She imagines a kitchen bright with daffodils, flooded with spring sunshine. She remembers her nan, who used to tell how Grandad brought her to an all-electric home. 'With fitted carpets throughout', Nan said. 'That's real love, that is.' She'll learn to cook like her nan. If only…

'What are you saying?' she asks him, tremulously, as if cajoling a butterfly to settle on her hand. Risking everything on those four words which might send him flying away into the blue. But:

'Will you marry me, Mary?' he asks.

'Oh yes, John, I will, I will!'

They stand, facing each other, contemplating the treasures that will so richly furnish their little home, their nest.

'Are you looking for something special?' The sales consultant has returned.

'We've found it,' he says.

Jenny Woodhouse

THE SPACES IN BETWEEN

'Now, Ginny takes first pick of vacation time, on account of her having the little ones.'

I knew for a fact that Ginny's kids were thirteen and fifteen – she told me that on my first day, two weeks ago. But I let it go and said nothing.

Una Roberts pointed to a row of pink stars. 'And Samuel, he always takes priority around Passover – that's like Easter to people of the Jewish persuasion.'

She made it sound like a tongue twister. And I would have laughed, but for her earnest expression.

'And he'll leave early on a Friday – in the winter months, you understand.' (Yellow stars, unbelievably.)

I could have told her that I did Comparative Religious Studies at High School, and that I understood very well indeed.

'Tajinder, you already know about (blue stars); and Mary-Beth likes to…' She paused and cleared her throat. 'Honour the *Old Ways* – she splits her days around the eight nature festivals.' Then she sighed and turned back to the wall planner.

'And how about you, Mrs Roberts?' I figured it was time I said something.

She let slip a little smile. 'Oh, I try to be flexible where I can – one has to be mindful that we are a multi-cultural society now.' She shifted round and stared at the array of stars and extended marker lines. I couldn't see an extra colour there, for either of us.

'Christmas, Easter, public holidays mainly – it's easier for me because I'm only ten minutes from home.'

I failed to see what difference this made to having time off work. But I stuck with my winning formula and just nodded.

'So anyway, Matthew, have a think about when you'd like your vacation time – no rush at all.'

I scanned the chart for gaps between stars and marker lines and thick red ink that shouted CONFERENCE and END OF MONTH FIGURES. I spied a space mid August and gazed upon it covetously.

'That's when I visit my mother,' she said. 'I just haven't had a chance to mark it up.' She plastered five green stars across the week, like barbed wire.

And we stood for a while, side by side, as if she were silently daring me to take my chances and pick again. I slowly extended a finger and she followed my lead, slapping the board like a flyswatter. July, August and September fell beneath her stubby arm, the flesh extending down into the top edge of October.

'Early June will suit me fine,' I said quietly, picking out the silver stars from the pot and readying the first one on the strip.

She glanced sideways at me, catching the corner of my smile. 'Oh no dear, that won't be possible. June we keep free wherever we can, just in case.'

And that was how I wound up taking my annual vacation in early November. And it naturally followed that I yearned for the sun and that meant a long journey. So the second year, when I weighed it all up, I figured there was little sense in going back to the job. After all, I was lower on the list than a week of 'just in case'.

And working in a café seemed the perfect thing to do while I was figuring out what to do next, which was where Old Davey had his bright idea at the end of an evening shift. The big room out back – Davey said it used to be a repair room when the café was some kind of big electrical shop. Well, that became the first little theatre this place ever had. And folks got to like it. So we needed more people and some local talent.

Well, one cool June morning, this woman breezes in, with her hair tied just so and one of those smart embroidered jackets on. And under her arm is a play she's just written, and she hands it to me confidently. Only she looks away as soon as I started to read it.

Three months later, we're sitting together at the side, watching the big performance, her hand in mine. And that, kids, is pretty much how I met your mother. And that is why you should take any job on offer, at the beginning. Because you never know quite where it's gonna lead.

And as the kids made a face and went outside to clear the tables, Martha stuck her head past the doorway and rolled her eyes. 'Are you coming through? Because we've got customers and I want to get this place cleaned before curtain up.'

Derek Thompson

TIME IS A FOUR-LETTER WORD

She sounds like a judge giving sentence. All she needs is a black cap and I'll be meeting Albert Pierrepoint in the near future.

'We've had all the tests back and there is no doubt that you have suffered a T.I.A. It's what is commonly known as a mini stroke.'

Her face is a mask of professional care as she follows up with a slight confident smile that doesn't reach her eyes, which are a stunning blaze of azure blue.

'I will prescribe some blood thinning drugs that will reduce the risk of fatty platelets being released into your blood stream. You should take this episode as a warning that you need to slow down; take more exercise; reduce stress levels. When was the last time you had a holiday?'

I was still taking in the stroke news and made no reply as she busied herself at her computer and handed me a prescription.

'You could experience some side effects. Feel confused and your balance may be affected. Please don't drive if this happens to you. Generally these side effects pass within a month or two, but if they persist we might have to consider changing the medication.'

So this is how the grim reaper looks, thirty plus in a soft linen suit with straightened blonded hair and those azure blue eyes. Every moment is precious and I am going to enjoy my retirement.

Rain cascading onto and through my almost waterproof anorak forced me into the only dry spot along the lonely cliff path. The day started well with a sunrise glowing red over the eastern hills throwing shards of shadows onto the satin soft damp grass surrounding the comfortable B&B. A good breakfast finishing off with my cocktail of tablets as prescribed. My plan, an easy walk on the coastal path for twelve miles. Up the track over Baggy Point, and down to the comfort of supper in the always cheerful atmosphere of the Red Barn. Then, in the twilight of this early autumn day, a comfortable further two miles to reach my friend's empty cottage.

As I ducked through the low empty doorway of the ruins of a shepherd's shelter the rising gale haunted the walls and crooned in the cracks between the dry stone walls.

'Red sky at night, shepherd's delight. Red sky in the morning shepherd's warning!'

Stripping off my outer layer the old countryman's ditty plays through my head.

In the dim light I see a smoke blackened ceiling and, in a dry corner, the cold ashes of a fire are evident. I am not the first to find this refuge. Dry wood from two splintered roof beams and my copy of the North Devon Gazette soon change the atmosphere. The fire splutters, smokes and finally blazes as I sit on the hard packed earthen floor. Coffee from my flask flushes the inner chill from my body and I look more closely at my surroundings. Nailed into a crack is the skull of a sheep and below etched into the stone

This sheep had vim and vigour

til I sent it to its maker

Amos French 1889

I find myself dozing - the bloody tablets sometimes have that effect on me - without really noticing that a man is standing on the far side of the fire that is now just embers.

'This is a good place to rest isn't it? I come here to get away from the pressures of my congregation. I saw you looking at the inscription. Poor soul now locked in hell. Murdered his wife and her lover. He hid here to avoid being arrested, but to no avail. People shunned him even after the police gave him his freedom. They were convinced he was guilty.'

The voice is deep with a resonance of the pulpit. In the half-light I see that my companion is a tall dark man with a lusty beard that envelopes his neck and chest. The long dark overcoat has a velvet sheen, but it is the eyes that absorb me: they reflect a deep azure blue in the dying embers of the fire. I pick up my half-empty flask.

'Can I offer you some coffee?'

'You're very kind, sir, but no thank you. I do not take stimulants.'

'My health won't permit me either. But this is decaffeinated.'

The eyes smile and he turns. 'The weather is improving so I bid you goodbye, sir. I have no doubt we will meet again soon.'

Although the sun now shines through the door opening, I feel cold and alone with only the soul of Amos French to keep me company.

Henry Kitchen

RIPENING

I am his peach.

I sit, taut, watching him smile as he walks the length of day, and when the light is orange, he comes, swooping in with the promise of plates and pillows.

His fingers stroke my skin and I start to melt, softening into the scent of my own juices.

Between his palms, I lower, like a breast after a sigh, sinking until my coat becomes comfortable, looser.

Flaccid.

He turns away. I sag. I watch him leave. My face turns to promise more, but my insides are browning. I shrink, I dry, I become powder, dusted with grey.

I am shocked to realise that to ripen is to rot.

I wait.

I hear, 'That one, that looks overripe.'

I think, 'Bite me.'

Martha Williams

THE COLLECTOR

'Oh for goodness sake, Mother, he's a famous lepidopterist, he identified hundreds of species of moth when he was working in the Amazonian basin, he… Oh hell!'

Sally stood in the telephone box and listened to the rain beating on the windows and the buzz in the telephone earpiece. She put the receiver back on the cradle and willed the phone to ring. 'Come on, Mother, I have obviously run out of money, dial one, four, seven, bloody, one. Get the number I called you on and ring me back! It isn't rocket bloody science.' Though, on reflection, where her Mother was concerned, it might as well be. Even with the idiot's guide Sally had painstakingly prepared for her she still couldn't work the DVD player. Now she didn't know where Sally was, other than that she was somewhere in Wales and on her way to interview somebody or other. Her Mother had raised absentminded dottiness to the level of an art form. Sally fumed for another ten minutes, then tried to call her mother through the operator and reverse the charges. The line was engaged. She was probably talking to her sister. Since Dad died, Mother had always turned to her sister for advice and solace. Sally thanked the operator and said she would try again later She had better get back on the road. There was nearly an hour's drive to this unpronounceable place near Ponty Pridd according to the Sat Nav.

'Dear me.' Glendowr Pugh was all sympathy as Sally related her tale.

'You have come to a strange place in foul weather and no one knows where you are. I almost expect...' The flash of lightning and rumble of thunder was eerily on cue '...special effects.' he concluded. He peered at Sally as though at a particularly unusual specimen and then said, 'Tea?'

While Pugh pottered in the kitchen, Sally meandered around the living room, peering into cases holding some of the exotic specimens that had been the foundation of Pugh's reputation. Yet, even as she gazed at the creatures she had come to see and write about, she felt that something was missing.

'No family, no photographs, no memories. My work is, sadly, my life.' Pugh had returned with a stained tray laden with an odd assortment of mugs, cups, saucers and plates. 'Ah, yes.' he said after examining the tray, 'tea.' He went back to the kitchen.

'More tea?'

'No thanks.' Sally had already drunk two and a bit cups. 'It is lovely tea, though.'

'I think the local water may be responsible.' Pugh was staring into his cup as though hoping to read something enlightening inside.

'May I use your bathroom?' Sally got to her feet and then found she was feeling rather wobbly. She fell back abruptly into her chair and then rebounded onto the floor where she lay face down.

Pugh regarded her prostrate body dispassionately. How kind of a benevolent Universe to send him such a perfect specimen to begin his new collection!

John D. Ritchie

SHOW ME THE MUMMY!

Ramses the First stared out of the palace window, surveying the vast, flat desert plain in the distance where his mausoleum was going to be. The sandy site was huge, stretching as far as the eye could see. It was awe-inspiring.

He couldn't help a surge of pride and excitement. This would finally silence his critics, especially those toffee-nosed Romans. This would show he was truly divine: a living God on Earth.

The sepulchre was going to be so large, so tall, so elaborate and richly decorated that even Ra himself would be jealous.

'Tell me again,' he instructed his two newly-acquired advisors. 'Tell me how grand and magnificent my burial building will be.'

The first stroked his beard and held up his hand, as if painting a picture in the very air. 'Mighty Pharaoh, it will be the most mind-blowing, wondrous, extraordinarily extravagant sight ever beheld by man's eyes. It will make The Hanging Gardens of Babylon look like a window box…'

'Compared with its majesty the Grand Library at Alexandria will seem a mere second-hand book stall…' his companion added.

'It will be so massive it will give the Colossus of Rhodes an inferiority complex and he'll rush to change his name to Titch,' they elaborated.

That's wonderful, Ramses thought. Gosh, it's going to be even better than I'd dreamt. I won't be facing eternity in standard accommodation after all - I'm upgrading to an executive tomb!

'It will take an army of slaves working round the clock some thirty years to complete it,' the duo pressed on expansively. 'It will use up every piece of stone in the land... extra chunks will have to be imported and shipped along the Nile.'

It would, they promised, still be drawing tourists in 3,000 years' time - and reaping benefits for the hospitality and trinket trades.

'Sounds amazing and just the sort of thing I'm looking for,' the Pharaoh conceded, but suddenly frowned, 'just, isn't it going to be a bit... expensive? The Royal treasury is a tad empty at the moment, what with the famines and the plagues and the compensation claims for all the flooding from that nasty business with the Red Sea parting.'

The two exchanged a knowing look that Ramses couldn't quite figure out.

'We thought you might say that, oh Mighty Ruler,' the lead advisor admitted, 'so we've come up with a plan.'

'A plan?'

'To pay for it all - a fiscal strategy,' advisor number 2 elucidated. 'A sure-fire way for you to cover the cost of all the building work and materials, and turn in a tidy profit.'

A profit! Great! I need a way of raising some dosh, Ramses thought happily. I like these two.

'We launch an investment opportunity - in the Royal household's name - for ordinary Egyptians to put their cash into the construction project. We offer all investors a 10 per cent return on their cash,' Beardy explained.

'With interest rates like that money will pour in,' his sidekick agreed. 'Before you know it, you'll be up to your regal eyeballs in gold.'

Wow! Brilliant! The Pharaoh was about to congratulate the geniuses when a thought struck him. 'But how do we pay the interest to the investors - when we don't have any cash to start with?'

'Ah, that's where the clever bit comes in,' the wise men said, tapping the sides of their noses. 'You use the cash that comes in from the second wave of investors to pay the original savers their interest. And money from the third wave to pay the second wave and so on…'

'And is that legal?' the Ruler asked.

'Oh yes, quite legal. A collateralized debt package - reverse securitized in a credit default swap. Standard banking practice. And if anyone raises any questions, you can always refer them to us… in the Holy Lands, where we'll be administering the whole operation for our normal 25% cut.'

Doubts banished, Ramses the First shook on it.

'What's this investment device called?' he enquired, pouring them all a deal-sealing drink.

'Some people call it a Persian Ponzie,' they told him, 'but in Jerusalem we prefer to think of it as a Sumerian shuffle.'

The Pharaoh breathed a sigh of relief. 'That's all right then,' he said, beaming. 'For a moment there I thought it might be one of those dreadful pyramid schemes…'

Iain Pattison

Congratulations! I blanch, knowing I'm impotent.

Derek Thompson

THE MAGIC NUMBER

Too cold to feel cold, and too numb to pick the pieces of glass from her pockets, Tabitha hunkered in a patch of windowed winter sun with Major the tomcat, slid her fingers into his marmalade fur, and waited.

The brutal easterly wind fought to follow her into the cabin, screaming down the chimney, pounding against the door, and hissing away all warm air that the small open fireplace tried to breathe into their squalid dwelling.

Away from the full force of the freezing coastal blasts, her ears and face began to defrost first; stinging, while her fingers still felt nothing but the passage of vibrations from a contented cat. She patiently pictured the glass in her pockets: mostly green, but today one more piece of blue, smoothed by tide and time 'til it gleamed from its dull pebble bed, whispering, 'Pick me, pick me. You see me, don't you?'

And now, gradually, the pain. In soft, warm cat fur, throbbing fingers thawed and burned, while Tabitha thought of sharp, smooth beach booty in the pockets of the worn, woollen coat that was made for a child of her mother's generation and told of poverty and hand-me-downs.

How many pieces now? Her fingers flexed. When she reached the magic number, Mother would return to help her care for poor Father. Slowly, stiffly, she removed the coat and emptied the pockets.

Coughing, Father said not to raise her hopes so, but Tabitha knew collecting the blue and green pieces would break the sea's curse. The colours of a mermaid's tail – messages from the sea that her mother was sending home. Tabitha understood, even if Father didn't. She had counted the scales on the picture of The Little Mermaid: two hundred. Mother was fighting the curse, shedding her tail. The sea would soon return her.

Major one-eyed the traitorous door that had permitted the icy winds to whistle through, then, with confident paws, quietly assumed his right to the woollen coat.

Rachel Carter

PERFECT IN PINK

'Jesus … what the hell's she got on?'

John looks round, then whispers, 'She's done a Jordan!'

The hotel's not my idea of a wedding venue. I can still smell this morning's bacon, and the pink heart-shaped balloons that decorate the room clash horribly with the orange and brown carpet. To give Sandie credit, she's worked hard on accessorising the room, and the pink of the balloons matches her overblown dress and veil exactly.

Sandie smiles at her groom and passes her bouquet to her ancient bridesmaid.

No competition there!

John nudges me. 'Look at the dog.'

Sandie's cairn terrier, its face almost obscured by a pink bow, is being cradled by a tubby man dressed in a John Travolta suit and pink cravat. He is sobbing.

I giggle. John prods me. I cover my mouth, bite my finger.

The vows are made. The dog handler sings 'Somewhere Over the Rainbow', then mops his tears.

John raises his eyebrows. I snigger, look away.

I see the video camera.

I twirl round and round, smooth my hands over my silk dress. I feel like Deborah Kerr in 'The King and I'.

Dad takes my hand and kisses it. 'You look like a princess, Sandie – a proper princess.' He hugs me. 'Your mum would have been proud.'

Kath puts down her bridesmaid's bouquet and straightens my veil. 'She'd have loved your dress and veil, Sand – she always was one for pink.'

'Thank you Auntie Kath – thank you for –'

'Ssh.'

Dad takes my arm. 'Come on, love. Let's crack on.'

Our guests turn round when we walk down the aisle. Everyone smiles. The heart shaped balloons look stunning – fifty-one for every year of Mum's life.

Somehow I say my vows. Cousin Pete, already red-faced from crying, sings 'Somewhere Over the Rainbow', dries his eyes, then walks over and hugs me.

'That one was for your mum, Sandie.'

Diane Simmons

RESISTANCE, 1943

His betrayer he never knew. The radio and explosives were quickly found. But neither stone-faced men in grey nor the terror of interrogation could break him. He breathed no word. Blindfolded, he sensed the green of the forest, the scent of the pines. Defiant to the end: 'Vive la France!'

Gill Garrett

SKIMMING

I flick my wrist and watch as the flat pebble slices its way through the air. The distinct arc of its flight is mirrored in the calm, silvery water of the pond. It's as if I'm seeing two pebbles on parallel journeys, or two mirrored pebbles on collision trajectory.

Their first skimmed contact is fleeting, but magical. A stunning clash of physics and chance, which leaves the surface of the water alive, dancing with a radiant glimmer of circular waves. Waves which sparkle as they flow outward, spreading the jubilation of the pebble's encounter.

I watch as the pebble rises again, as if it has been elated by the water's touch, and not simply spinning onward in accordance with Newton's third law. It resumes flight, but its course has been deviated, the direction of its journey forever altered.

It again sails high above its mirrored self, seemingly unaware, or uncaring that its flight is on a new vector. It leaves the ripples caused by the contact far behind, although it is obvious that the energetic promise of its early flight has been dampened, obvious that its momentum has been slowed by its dalliance with the surface, obvious too that it will fall to skim again.

The second contact is slower, firmer, almost more deliberate. It seems as though either the reflection clings longer to the pebble, or maybe the pebble seeks to immerse itself further into the cool mystery of the pond.

And once again its onward path is deviated, subtly changed by the experience of contact. The pebble skims upward, but its motion has now become laboured, as if it is fighting against the physics which force it away, or as though it has become suddenly confused by the new tangent of its journey.

Then three, four, five contacts in rapid succession. Each more inevitable than the last. Each reaffirming the growing familiarity between pebble and reflection, each seeming to cause the pebble to question the purpose of its onward flight. So that after every fleeting caress the pebble struggles harder to break free, to return to its journey, although the direction of its original path is now long forgotten.

I watch in those final, frantic moments, as distinctions are blurred, as the pebble and its reflection succumb to the inevitable. The ripples caused by those rapid collisions are close together, intermingled. No longer a jubilant wave but a chaotic weave of shimmering distortions which are impossible to ignore, and which scar the surface of the pond long after the pebble has fallen into the water's final embrace.

After the pebble is lost I stand and watch the undulations as they heave and clash, waiting, anxious for the surface of the pond to realign, to return to its former tranquil, mirror state. Waiting for all to become placid and calm, for it to recover from the chaotic ripples caused by the erratic flight of the pebble.

Berating the interference of the wind, I stand and watch because I need to see, need to witness the pond's surface finally settle. I need to know that life has not been permanently marred by those magical collisions of physics and chance, of pebble and reflection, of you and me.

James Coates

THAT GIRL

He pretended not to look and I pretended not to see. Yet we both knew he was looking at her as she sauntered straight out of the pages of a magazine and down the street. I knew what he was thinking, but I resisted the urge to say: *As if! She's way out of your league!*

Later, when we quarrelled about whose turn it was to wash the dishes, I told him, 'I saw you looking at that girl,' but he just looked at me as if I were mad.

Sam Payne

THE COPPICE

It was still snowing.

The old farmhouse door shoved open. Bjorn Martinsson gazed out across his land to a small coppice. He used to tend it and gather hazel for fencing. But a long time ago now. He turned and scratched his stubble, watching as the snow thickened on the tractor in the yard.

Martinsson strode over to it. The cab windows steamed as he tried the starter. After a few turns the engine spluttered into life. The shroud of snow vibrated steadily off the machine. He smiled, left it running and went to the coop for some eggs.

Sitting in the ramshackle kitchen he finished breakfast and stared at the battered armchair. Hanna's chair. He wondered why he thought of her now. She had gone five years ago. Perhaps he was getting old and missed the company, her sitting there, always making something, always doing with her busy fingers. But then, her busy voice. Yak, yak, yak. Like he was a female companion, interested in dropped stitches and needles! And she not remotely interested in his tales from the tavern nor in what he felt was his due: open legs and an embracing of his manhood. And then the nagging. They had all done that. But still…

He hitched the small trailer to the tractor and headed off to the coppice. After clearing the snow he found the marker stone. He hacked at the frozen earth and dug down very carefully until he heard a dull thud. He eased the box into the trailer.

Yes, that will do nicely. She was back in her chair. Arranged. Bone silent. No sign now of the needle he had plunged into her eye. He told her a tale, then said that tomorrow Greta would be the first to join her.

Michael Kirby

Last human, online. Then instant message.

Derek Thompson

TRACKING ELEPHANTS

'Tenineightsevensixfifour-'

'Slow down, Rajiv!'

'OK, Auntie, but I really want to press the button — like in the movies.'

'Does there have to be a countdown?'

'Yes — like a rocket!'

'In which case you should do it properly. You need to count down the seconds, which is a lot slower.'

'Ten-'

'And you should start by saying "T minus" because that's what they use for real launches.'

Sucheta was regretting her decision to bring her nephew into work. Her sister had thought it might help spark Rajiv's interest in science. Sucheta had some calibration runs booked with the synchrotron, but Rajiv had shown little interest in protein structures. He was, however, excited by the facility's main building, a circular structure that housed the synchrotron, a flying saucer that had somehow parked itself discreetly in the English countryside. Its medical and materials science applications held no interest for him, but he was very taken with the idea of the synchrotron as a particle ray gun or some kind of futuristic propulsion system.

'T minus ten... nine-eight-seven-six-'

'Still too fast. Try counting elephants.'

'What?'

'Pardon,' Sucheta corrected. 'Saying "elephant" makes the interval around a second. T-minus ten elephant, nine elephant-'

'Shouldn't you say "elephants"? We did plurals at school.'

Sucheta's glare sent a message. Rajiv got it.

Besides being his aunt, what did she really know about children? How was she supposed to know that you shouldn't let kids have energy drinks? Her sister had never said anything, nor had any of her colleagues with children ever let slip this vital information. The countdown seemed superfluous: he was already in orbit. She certainly couldn't return him home until he'd landed.

'T minus ten-elephant-nine-elephant-eight-elephant-'

'Rajiv, that's a stampede not a countdown!'

'Auntie, I have the best elephants! They are fast.'

'Let's take turns. You take the numbers, I'll herd the elephants. And let's start from five.' She did not believe his anticipation could be contained for a whole ten seconds.

'T minus five...'

'… elephant, …'

'… four…'

'… elephant, …'

'… three …'

'… elephant, …'

'… two…'

'… elephant, …'

'… one…'

'… elephant….'

'Blast off!'

Now she could start calibrating. About an hour since the drink? Probably another hour to go.

Kevlin Henney

WENDY THE WATER BUFFALO

Wendy our water buffalo is blue. You never saw such a sad-looking creature, eyes as mournful as a plaster Madonna. We brought her from Romania. There's plenty of rain here in West Wales, but I worry she's pining. She pulled carts, ploughed fields, now she sits all day looking lost. It's not all bad news: she gives us great mozzarella.

Sarah Hilary

A GOOD DYING

'Tickets please.'

The girl lifted her huge carpet bag onto the table and started rummaging, 'Shit, it's in here somewhere.'

The guard rolled his eyes, holding on to a seat to steady himself. The girl brushed her long henna-red hair back, then attempted, and failed, to blow the stray strands away from her face.

She first placed an antique silver rose bowl and a bright green shower cap in the shape of a frog carefully on the table.

'Oh, good grief,' whispered the guard.

The girl wiped her brow on the velvet sleeve of her maroon dress. She then lifted both arms into the air, shaking them in an attempt to move the sleeves up her arm. Bangles jingled, rings sparkled. The guard smelled rose water.

A jade grotesque, what appeared to be a cheese and pickle sandwich, a can of ready-mixed gin and tonic, a teddy bear key-ring, cough medicine.

'Aaargh, where is it?' she said. 'Deep breaths.' Eyes framed in thick black eye makeup looked to the heavens.

The guard plucked at the front of his shirt trying to get some air flow.

The girl dived headlong back into the bag. A flat cap; black notebook; chocolate muffin; silenced .22 calibre Ruger; train ticket.

'Here it is,' she said. 'Oh!'

The guard was running out of the rear of the empty carriage, ticket machine bouncing off his hip and the seats. She shrugged her shoulders and meticulously placed the items back in the bag. The squeak of the brakes and the announcer declared they had arrived at Exeter Station. She loped out of the station.

The girl checked the address in her notebook. Satisfied, she walked up the empty drive. The old man looked up as she walked around the corner of the bungalow.

A red rose of blood grew on the old man's white shirt, followed a microsecond later, by the sound of two rounds entering his chest and the soft tinkle of brass shell cases falling on the patio stones.

The girl sighed. A sad satisfied sigh. There was a 'Wills and Kate' mug on the patio table. She tipped the tea into the flower bed and wiped it out with the hem of her dress. The girl placed the mug in her bag and left for the station.

Back on the train she consulted her notebook while devouring her cheese sandwich. Without looking she retrieved the can of gin and tonic from her bag and downed half of it. She held her hand in front of her. Still steady; after a year still steady. What did that mean?

The house in Bristol was a terraced, red brick building. She looked at her watch and waited in the bus shelter over the road. A bus stopped, blocking her view. She waved it on.

A blue car pulled off the drive. She stood, clomped across the road and around the back of the house. The back door was open. She made her way to the stairs. She climbed. Front bedroom. In the dressing table mirror the reflection of a man asleep. She crept in, avoiding the tubes, wires and host of mobility equipment. He was on his side facing away from her. She placed the cold muzzle of the suppressor against the nape of his neck. She shot him in the back of the head with a single soft nosed round. No exit wound. No noise, apart from the top slide of the automatic clicking backward then forward.

Gently she moved the man on to his back. No pulse. There was a spoon left on a tray from dinner. She picked it up and wiped the soup on her dress. It went into the bag. She caught the last train to London.

The girl stepped onto a narrow boat and slipped through the small door in the stern. It was dusk so she flicked on the lamp just inside the door. One by one she placed the items from the bag on the many shelves, fitting them in where she could. There was barely enough room.

Spoon, mug, rose bowl, teddy bear key-ring, shower cap, grotesque were all placed on the shelves. She booted up her laptop. She had mail.

Dear Dignity,

We are need of your services. My wife has Parkinsons and we are in agreement. Please contact us as soon as possible.

NH

'No rest for the righteous,' she said to the photograph of her mother on the desk.

Alastair Keen

GREENHAYES

'Christ, what was that?'

Frank doesn't answer but turns over, pulling the duvet with him.

I roll out of bed and peek through the blinds. 'Sounded like a car back-firing.'

'Not on Greenhayes. There aren't any old bangers around here.'

I scan the cul-de-sac, looking for any sign of movement, but it's all quiet. The mock-tudor houses stand in a row and our bay window offers a good view. I notice movement on the porch next door. It would be a foolish burglar trying to gain entry at the front. Reaching for my glasses, I see more clearly. There's a naked woman slumped on the doormat. Her tapered legs stretch to the step and her skin's all pearly in the moonlight.

'Well, I never!' The woman hugs her knees, trying to hide her breasts the size of honeydews. 'It's Jenny. Herman must've chucked her out.'

'I knew that marriage was never going to last.'

'But it's the middle of the night and she's got nothing on.' I grab Frank's dressing gown and tie the belt around my waist, throwing the other robe over my shoulder.

'Blimey, what a woman!' Frank's at the window - now he knows there's something worth watching. I stand beside him and we see Jenny shivering. 'You can't go interfering.'

'I'm only going to lend her my robe.'

'Herman went off his head when I cut a few inches off his precious Leylandii. You don't want to make an enemy of him.'

'I can't leave Jenny stuck on the porch like that. I'll never get a wink of sleep if I don't help her.'

I leave the house, my slippers clip-clopping as I walk to the boundary. The night is clear but the damp air clings. Standing on tiptoe, I peer over the wall. She sees me and scurries through the shrubs. Passing over the robe I notice her fingers are like ice. She pulls a smile, but looks set to burst into tears.

'Thank you.' Jenny's swollen top lip makes it hard for her to speak.

'Might stop you getting a cold – I'd invite you back, but Frank says no. Won't hear of it after that last row he had with Herman.'

'It's okay.' She struggles to get her arms into the sleeves. 'Herman will let me in soon.'

'Okay then.'

I still can't sleep in spite of my good deed, and, when it's time to get up, I'm like a dishrag. Limping to the window, I draw the blinds and there's no sign of Jenny. She must've found refuge somewhere. When I get downstairs, there's a parcel on the back porch. I peel back the brown paper and there's my robe all fluffy and warm from the tumble dryer. There was no need to wash and return it so promptly. I find an envelope nestling by the collar, and inside there's a 'thank you' note from Jenny. She's signed her name in loopy handwriting, and at the bottom, there's a smiley face. Only this smiley face has a black eye. I wonder if it's a coded message for help and I think about Jenny trapped in Herman's executive home like a modern day Cinderella, but without a prince in sight. I look again at the smiley face and decide it's not a black eye just a blot from the ballpoint pen.

Gail Aldwin

10:05 – 11:05

10:05 am, Walcot Street. The Christmas decorations are dangling and pointless in January daylight. She waits for him at the bottom of the steps. A thin band of ice contracts around her chest. She has showered, shaved her legs with care and doused her body with the scent of hope against hope; but everything else she's put on is slightly wrong. Her skirt is too short for knees this old, and it won't pull down to cover the spread of her thighs. At least the inappropriate attempt at cleavage is protected from the chill by her sensible coat. He said he'd be there at 10 o'clock, and once again he isn't. Her final chance for happiness in life has already lost its fake fizz, like an abandoned glass of Cava on the morning after. Welcome to the New Year, same as the old year.

Someone has etched a hopscotch grid in pink chalk along the opposite pavement. It wasn't there yesterday, but now it is. This isn't a random childish thing. It smacks of adult strangeness and determination – or concept art – not ending after a meagre ten squares or so, but extending along the street and out of sight. She can't tell where it finishes without leaving their appointed meeting place. And then she might miss him when he arrives. She must remain where she is until he appears.

She practices breathing, deliberately tries to slow the speed of her heart and lower her blood pressure. She must learn not to care – five minutes is only five minutes; it's hardly late at all. It's silly to worry about such fragments of time when life is so full of the stuff. What is an hour, or a whole day even? Whether it's wasted or used, how much difference does that make to the end result? She doesn't like her own logic. If nothing ever matters, then why get out of bed?

How long do you wait for something before you admit to yourself that it won't happen? As a child, she could wait all winter for snow. When it didn't arrive she would wait all summer for the chance of it again. She tries to remember when she gave up being that patient, when adulthood took hold and a few minutes in a queue could cause her to flee.

She paces slowly, fiddles with her gloves and sings 'He who would valiant be...' to herself inside her head. School hymns, dusty bibles, playground rituals, being free of all responsibility and choice. To wait or leave?

She calls his mobile three times. At first it's engaged, and then when she tries later both times it goes straight to voicemail. He can't find a parking spot, he's been called into the office on his day off, he's lying dead in a ditch or been abducted by aliens. It's meaningless to speculate, but speculation is what she has time for right now. She could window-shop, she supposes, but she doesn't want a bicycle, to paint a pot, frame a picture, repair a sewing machine, or purchase knee-high leather boots first sold in 1964. She would never have worn them the first time around, and it's too late to start now.

She looks at the hopscotch markings – without getting past square one – while she waits for him to arrive. Perhaps they don't finish at the end of the street at all. Maybe they go all the way around the corner into the London Road. Where to then? She tries to believe she could hop from Walcot through Wiltshire, then on and on beyond the Home Counties and out to the Essex coastline, following the squares of pink chalk lines.

11:05 am Walcot Street. She begins to skip the hopscotch grid, not caring whether anyone watches her progress. Each footfall jolts numbed toes. She begins a journey; each fresh square contains a new possibility of happiness. None will ever be final. She no longer waits for him, her convictions dangling and pointless in January daylight.

Pauline Masurel

THE LOVING PLACEMENT OF FISH

'Emily.'

The policewoman is back. The hospital pillow crackles as Emily rolls her head away.

'Tell me about Leo Tymoshenko.'

Words form ragged queues around the firestorm scars in Emily's brain. 'He was my port...porter, when I had radiotherapy.'

The malignant melamine or melodeon or something had sent cells like junk mail from a mole to her brain. No-one had seen it begin to gnaw, because Emily Linklater was unmanned. No-one had holiday-romance-paperbacked her forty-something body, and noticed.

'Radiology for MRI?' His tanned face was lopsided, his accent exotic. His badge had been difficult to read upside down. 'It's Leo.'

The trolley lurched over a bump into the lift. 'Are you Polish?'

'No, no, I'm from Ukraine. Leonid Tymoshenko. And you are—Mrs Linklater.'

'Miss. Emily.'

'Emily.' That voice again. There is an antiseptic taste in her mouth, from the anaesthetic.

The warmth starts to fill Emily up, with the memory of his soft voice, stretching vowels into strange shapes. His pink tongue licking his lips. 'He was my porter. He was kind, sociable.'

'So, he was friendly?'

He had been there, behind the curtain when the clichés had fluttered around her head like flies. *You can beat the odds, are in the right place, can get the best care.* After the first treatments her speech would stumble around blind, picking up words at random. So Leo would talk, about the Ukraine, about living in England.

'The first round of treatment affected my speak—speech, but the tumour shrink—shrank. Then I had radiotherapy.' Death rays, Leo called it, as they bombarded her, using tattoos on her scalp. Days had folded into nights and she had drifted onto the high care unit.

'Emily.'

The policewoman has a ring on her finger: someone sees her private places, would see an invading darkness before it becomes cancer. 'Can you recall any occasion when he touched you?'

The memory was like a soft toy, to be hugged. He was there, whispering, hands rubbing her breasts, tugging at her nightgown. She had lifted herself up so he could free her, explore her. His tongue tasted like coffee, was hot and firm. She could feel him inside, sensations growing like rainbow flashes, her hair, hovering around her shoulders and drifting to the floor.

They were making love on her parents' front lawn, her father mowing carefully around them, leaving the shape of a vulva in the green stripes. His body was furrowing hers, ploughing her broad white body. He put a hand over her mouth when she tried to speak, so the words bounced around inside her skull: *I love you, I love you...*

'Emily.'

She must have been asleep. 'What? I didn't hear the question.'

Did Leo Tymoshenko ever kiss you, or touch you in a sexual way?'

'I wanted him to. I love him.' *Leo.*

'You understand why you are in hospital?'

'I have a speech problem, but I'm not brain damned—damaged.'

'You were brought in because you were having a miscarriage.'

She remembers now: a scarlet fish carved out of liver. It had slipped out of Emily's body in Casualty, after her belly had twisted all day.

Leo. Leo had placed his baby inside her and somehow she had dropped it.

'I suppose all the treatment killed it. It killed my hair.' She wasn't sad for a baby that was only a fish, and a tumour that had grown into love in her brain. 'Can I see Leo, now?'

'I'm sorry, Emily, but Leo Tymoshenko has been arrested.'

The words ooze into Emily's brain past the pockmarks of the treatments.

'Arrested?'

'For rape.'

'Rape?' The word feathers out of her.

'He was in your room, when you were unconscious.' The policewoman leans forward. 'It's a matter of consent. There was evidence there, of sexual activity.'

Whiskery kisses, the hairy skin, hard knees as he pushed her legs apart. She did remember him climbing down, muttering something, words of tenderness, gratitude, love. He had gone to the sink and pulled out paper towels. His hands were rough, cleaning her private parts, pulling her nightgown down, the blankets up. A wave of tenderness swept the policewoman's words away, and she closed her eyes again.

Rebecca Alexander

CITADEL

The door had not even finished wheezing shut, but I was already on the balcony.

I hadn't paused to admire the two-star furnishings, instead I headed for the five-star view.

Athens was laid out before me in the dark: scattered diamonds on velvet, but above it all, hovering in its own glow, was the Acropolis. I stared at it and felt its gravity.

It was dark as I walked the streets and darker still on the hillside, but I didn't care. My eyes were fixed upwards to the horizon, pulling me forward.

As I neared it, the illusion of the columns floating in the night sky grew stronger. The light streamed up their length and led them up into the heavens, aiming them at the stars.

The closer I drew, the more I expected the dream to evaporate, but it didn't. If anything, it became more fixed, more real. As I arrived at the base of the structure I realised why. I could see no spotlights. No lamps of any kind. The light that was creating the effect came from no obvious source.

I took the final steps into the building and felt power run through me. It was pure God-light that was illuminating this building; the result of thousands of years of belief.

I could feel them swarming around me: Aphrodite and Athena, Dionysus and Demeter, Hera, Hermes and Zeus.

All was light.

Calum Kerr

THE FLASH-FICTION SW WRITERS

Gail Aldwin lives in Dorset and enjoys writing short stories and flash fiction as relief from the slog of completing a novel. Her work appears in online publications including Paragraph Planet, Five Stop Story, Ink Sweat and Tears and CafeLit. Three print anthologies coming to press in 2012 contain examples of her writing. Gail has a regular column in What the Dickens? Magazine that answers writers' questions. She also blogs about all things literary at: http://gailaldwin.wordpress.com

Rebecca Alexander is a fiction writer and poet living in North Devon. She left a career as a psychologist, listening to people's extraordinary stories, to write her own. Her first novel, Borrowed Time, was a runner up in the Mslexia competition, and attracted a literary agent. She blogs at http://witchwayblogspotcom.blogspot.co.uk/

Hazel Bagley is from North Wiltshire and has been a member of a local writing group for seven years. She has entered short story competitions several times but this is the first time she's tried flash fiction. She works as a tour guide in Bath.

Jennifer Bell lives in a little ramshackle cabin in North Dorset. Her stories have appeared in print and online including Kasma SF, The Pygmy Giant, Dogmatika and others. Her website is at www.bellstories.co.uk

Richard Bond was born, lives and will probably die in Bristol, although he has plans before then. He started writing short stories and flash fiction about two years ago when he realised it was more rewarding than yet more opening chapters of unfinished novels. Richard was a runner up in the Fish Flash Fiction prize 2011 and was published in the Fish Anthology

Margaret Bradshaw lives in S Devon; has a love/hate relationship with creative writing; has self-published one poetry pamphlet; and enjoys canoeing.

Rosalind Browne runs an old fashioned Hardware shop based in East Devon. She has been writing for, oooh… about five minutes, having discovered Flash Fiction via her friend and business partner Alastair Keen (also featured in this list) she hopes she hasn't trodden on his toes! She believes that old wine is better than young and hopes that other people feel the same.

Joanna Campbell of Gloucestershire, writes short stories all day at home in the Cotswolds, with three cats and occasional bowls of cereal for company. She has been published in various magazines and anthologies. In 2010 and 2012 she was shortlisted for both the Fish and the Bridport Short Story Prizes. In 2010 she was shortlisted for the Bristol Short Story Prize. She is currently writing a novel as well as trying to be her husband's company secretary. She hopes she is a better writer than she is a secretary, as does her husband.

Rachel Carter, from North Devon, is a mother of three and co-owner of a surf shop in Croyde. She writes short stories and flash fiction (some of which are published with Ether Books), and takes part in the online Friday Flash community. She has studied 13 Open University modules, and has a diploma in literature and creative writing. Whilst putting together this anthology she is supposed to be completing an honours degree and a VAT return. She blogs at http://rachelcarter.me/

James Coates lives in Bournemouth, Dorset. He has been writing for about a year. One of his stories was recently featured in American flash fiction magazine 'Stanley the Whale'.

Josephine Corcoran, who currently lives in Trowbridge, West Wiltshire, returned to writing in 2010, after a ten-year gap spent raising two fantastic children. Her work is published, broadcast (on BBC R4) and performed. http://josephinecorcoran.wordpress.com

Melanie Doherty lives in South Gloucestershire. She has had the itch to write from a very early age. In past years, several of her short stories for children were published in magazines, but more recent times allowed very little space for her inner storyteller. For her, this chance to attempt a piece of flash fiction was a timely prompt to let it spread its wings again! Melanie blogs at: http://bookishnature.wordpress.com/

Gill Garrett lives in Cheltenham in Gloucestershire and writes poems and short stories. A lecturer in a previous existence, she now supports care home residents with life story work and creative writing.

Gilly Goldsworthy, from Exeter, completed a Diploma in Creative Writing with the Open University in 2011. She intends to write fiction and is slowly writing her first novel but indulges her passion for travel writing at lucidgypsy.wordpress.com

Kevlin Henney from Bristol writes shorts and flashes and drabbles of fiction and articles and books on software development. His fiction has appeared online and on tree with Litro, Fiction365, Dr. Hurley's Snake-oil Cure, The Fabulist, The Liminal, New Scientist and FlashStories.net. He blogs at asemantic.netand tweets as @KevlinHenney.

Tania Hershman from Bristol has had flash stories published online and in print and broadcast on Radio 4. Her second book, a collection of 56 very short stories, My Mother Was An Upright Piano: Fictions, is published in May by Tangent Books. www.taniahershman.com

Muriel Higgins is a retired teacher of English as a foreign language and text-book writer. Born and educated in Scotland, she has lived in several countries overseas and moved to Dorset in 2005.

Sarah Hilary is a Bristol-based award-winning short story scribbler, published in Smokelong Quarterly, the Fish Anthology, and by the Crime Writers' Association (CWA). In 2011, she won an Honourable Mention in the Tom-Gallon Trust Award. Sarah blogs at www.sarah-crawl-space.blogspot.com. Her agent is Jane Gregory.

Claire Huxham lives in Weston-super-Mare, North Somerset, and has been writing since 2009; her fiction, non-fiction and poetry can be found in places like Metazen, The Foundling Review, Danse Macabre and The Hollywood News. She lectures in English at a local FE college and is particularly keen on Buffy, cats, sushi and cheese. She blogs here: clairejoannehuxham.blogspot.co.uk/

Mandy James from Bristol has been writing for as long as she can remember. She has short stories in many anthologies and with Ether Books.

Her novel, Righteous Exposure, was released by Crooked Cat Publishing, in February of this year. http://crookedcatpublishing.com/our-books/righteous-exposure-by-a-k-james 2012. http://mandykjameswrites.blogspot.co.uk/2012/04/when-wind-is-in-west.html

Alastair Keen is a former soldier, ex-RSPCA Inspector and was for a while Director of Operations of the Irish SPCA, amongst other things. He is now the part owner of a hardware store (think fork 'andles), Open University Student, chicken whisperer and writer. He is a featured writer on flash fiction world .com and National Flash Fiction Day. His fiction can be found on Pygmy Giant, flash fiction world.com, The Rusty Nail Mag, Etherbooks, Urban Fantasist.com amongst other places. He is presently pinging his novel 'Unnecessary Suffering' to agents and publishers. A future ambition is to train one of his rare breed bantams for military and law enforcement purposes, if only they would pay attention for two minutes…

Calum Kerr is a writer, editor, lecturer and Director of National Flash-Fiction Day. He lives in Southampton and teaches at the University of Winchester. His stories have appeared in a number of places including Bugged, Flash: The International Journal of the Short Short Story, Shoestring, The Pygmy Giant, Litro and Apollo's Lyre. Last year he had 22 flash-fictions featured on Radio 4's PM and iPM programmes. He has been writing and blogging a flash-fiction every day for a year at flash365.blogspot.com and his self-published pamphlet, 31, is available from www.calumkerr.co.uk and on Kindle from Amazon. His new pamphlet, Braking Distance, will be published by Salt at the beginning of May 2012.

Michael Kirby is from Chudleigh in Devon and has been writing 'longish' short stories for about five years. One of these stories was long-listed for the Fish prize. He is at last editing his own twenty odd year-old Sci Fi novel. This is his first try at Flash fiction.

Henry Kitchen lives North Devon near Holsworthy. He writes short stories as relaxation from voluntary work

Lesley Lees, from Plymouth, Devon, has just started to write flash fiction but has been writing poetry for the last few years.

Iris Lewis is a short story writer and poet living in Gloucestershire. After a management career in the education and healthcare sectors she is now able to devote more time to creative writing. She has only recently started to submit her material for publication. As a new writer she is delighted that she has been successful in both having her poetry and flash fiction accepted for inclusion in anthologies.

Pauline Masurel lives in South Gloucestershire. She is a gardener and writer of short and tiny fictions. Her website is at www.unfurling.net.

Louisa Adjoa Parker is a poet and black history writer who lives in West Dorset. Her first poetry collection 'Salt-sweat and Tears' was published in 2007. Her work has appeared in various anthologies and magazines, including the Forward Prize collection; Wasafiri; Envoi and Ouroboros. She has written books and exhibitions about the presence of African and Caribbean people in Dorset. Louisa first wrote flash fiction as part of a BBC project 'Made in the South' in 2009 and has continued writing short stories since then. She is currently researching the presence of African American GIs in Dorset in 1944 as well as working on her second poetry collection and her first novel. Louisa is co-editor of 'Dorset Voices' – a collection of local prose, poetry and photography, published this April by Roving Press.

Iain Pattison from Bristol is a full-time author, creative writing tutor and competition judge. His short stories have been widely published in the UK and the United States and broadcast on BBC Radio 4. His book Cracking The Short Story Market (Writers Bureau Books) is a best seller. www.iainpattison.com

Sam Payne lives in Plymouth and is a full time mum, part time student and a part time trolley dolly on the great British Railway. She has just completed a Diploma in Creative Writing with the Open University and is now studying for a degree in English Literature. Sam blogs at http://chasintheplot.wordpress.com/

Deborah Rickard from Bristol, has had short stories published in women's magazines and online. She started writing flash fiction in 2011, has enjoyed various competition successes and has been shortlisted for the 2012 Fish Flash Fiction Award. For her, flash fiction opens the mind to a moment and keeps it open …

John D. Ritchie lives in North-east Wiltshire and has been writing flash Fiction since 2005. He has had stories published in the following anthologies 'HeavyGlow 2005-2007', 'DoorKnobs and Body Paint 2008' and the 'Best of Everyday Fiction 2008'. He is frequently found, these days, in Five Minute Fiction.

Diane Simmons, from Bath, started writing just over five years ago when she embarked on an Open University creative writing course. She has not stopped writing since and now has a Diploma in Literature and Creative Writing (with Distinction) from the Open University. She enjoys entering writing competitions and her successes include runner up in the SHE/This Morning short story competition (2009), top ten finalist in Woman and Home's 2010 competition and 1st, 2nd and 3rd place in The Frome Festival competition for local writers in 2011, 2010 and 2009 respectively. She has recently had a story published in The Yellow Room magazine. This is her first flash fiction success.

Rin Simpson is a Bristol-based freelance journalist and creative writer, and founder of The Steady Table writers' group.

Sarah Snell-Pym, a Gloucester-based writer, loves flash fiction writing ever since she found the Friday Flash hashtag on twitter. Her writing varies in length and style ranging from kids' poetry to the darkly political. Website http://www.snell-pym.org.uk/sarah/

Natalia Spencer is a new writer from Bristol and a Creative Writing student at Bathspa University. Four years ago, despite never having used a computer before, she began blogging and this became the impetus for the development of her poetry and prose fiction.

Derek Thompson is a writer and humorist living in West Cornwall. He writes fiction and non-fiction, but flash fiction holds a special place in his heart. As the saying goes: "Sometimes less is more." His blog lives at: http://www.alongthewritelines.blogspot.com and you're all invited.

Brendan Way from North Devon has been writing things ever since he learnt how to handle a pen. He has been writing flash fiction, mainly as part of blog team The Flashnificent 7, for considerably less time. His work for them can be found here, http://flashnificent7.blogspot.co.uk/, but, if you're not in the mood for a short story, you can always check out some sarcastic pedantry of his here: http://thebrendanway.blogspot.co.uk/.

Martha Williams lives and writes in Cornwall, on a big, wet rock overlooking the Atlantic. She has a selection of flash and short stories published in print and online, and blogs at http://marthawilliams.org

Jenny Woodhouse retired to Bath where she has been writing seriously since she took an Open University diploma in literature and creative writing in 2007-9. Previously she specialised in papers and policies. Her preferred genre is short stories, which are growing shorter and evolving into flash fiction. She has been shortlisted on a number of occasions and hopes one day to graduate from bridesmaid to publication.

THE READERS

Gail Aldwin loves reading and writing flash fiction during snatches of the day when she's not required as a parent, partner or teacher. She blogs at: gailaldwin.wordpress.com

Cath Barton is a singer, writer and photographer who lives in South Wales and is published here and there.

Kay Beer loves to read and write, is a recently published short story writer but still an aspiring novelist, because she's fascinated by the things people do in their pursuit of love. Can be found rambling at:
http://www.1lovelife.blogspot.co.uk/

Natalie Bowers is a fledgling writer, perpetual student and professional volunteer, who lives in Hampshire with her husband, two children and a ukulele.

Georgina Cambridge, from South Ashford, is studying her Bachelors of Arts in English Literature and has enjoyed reading since she was Four.

Liz Coleman is originally from Scotland but now lives in Ireland. In a previous working life,

Liz used to read writing competition entries as part of her job. Now she writes and enters too!

Peter Domican, from Welwyn Garden City, is a new flash fiction writer who believes in choosing his words carefully

Lorena Hodgson lives in Fenland, home-educates her family, and enjoys reading anything when she gets the chance.

Anouska Huggins, from Newcastle, is a reluctant accountant by day, a student of writing and literary things by night, and in between is a prolific gin drinker.

Linda Southern, presently living in Scotland, is an Open University Student, a primary school administrator and loves to read.

Tracy Tyrrell works to support the development of English teaching across four Bolton secondary schools. She is a compulsive reader and an aspiring writer. She hangs around on Twitter as MrsT and blogs at: http://mrstwritesinclemency.blogspot.co.uk

Kay Warner, a mum to 3 girls from the Forest of Dean, loves reading. She will try reading anything but likes a good thriller or adventure - with her favourite authors being James Patterson and Clive Cussler.

Amanda Warren, from Hampshire, is a big manga reader and an aspiring screenwriter

Elizabeth Welsh is a freelance editor for a number of university presses and publishing companies worldwide. She writes poetry and short fiction and has been published in numerous print and online collections. She also has a chapter in a forthcoming collection on New Zealand short story writer, Katherine Mansfield. She blogs about all things literary here: ewelsh.wordpress.com

Martha Williams lives and writes on a big, wet rock overlooking the Atlantic. She has a selection of flash and short stories published in print and online, and blogs at marthawilliams.org